Just Die

E. Alan Fleischauer

FIRST EDITION, JANUARY 2021

Copyright 2021 by E. Alan Fleischauer

ISBN-13: 978-1-7335940-6-6

Just Die

1

JAKE SILVER SAT BOLT UPRIGHT, the hackles rising on the back of his head. He had no idea where he was. He blinked. Last thing he remembered, it had been dark outside. Now the sun was streaming in through a dust-streaked window, illuminating the fact that he was in a strange bed. At least he knew it was August 24—or was it?

The ding of a monitor on a stand next to his bed gave him the first clue as to his location. The second was a hefty woman clad in blue scrubs, bursting through the door with a scowl on her face. "Oh, no, Mr. Silver, you have to lie down," she admonished. "You've had a stroke, and you need to rest."

Jake's head jolted forward, his eyes wide. "Dee uoo ssas um strrrrrle?"

The nurse placed her hands on Jake's shoulders. "Yes, a stroke, which is why you're talking gibberish." She pushed him firmly back against the pillows.

Jake looked around the room and shook his head in dismay. "Wagu-lerl-er, wag la-ur." A single tear rolled down his cheek.

"Did you say water?" the nurse asked, more kindly.

Jake nodded.

"I'm very sorry, but Dr. Jordan says you can only have ice chips." She turned and walked out of the room, leaving Jake to wonder whether she was actually going to fetch the ice chips or leave him to die of thirst.

The last thing he remembered, he was at Ike's, his favorite restaurant. He was with Beth Ann, his fiancée, and a few of his best friends. He'd just sold his financial planning business for millions, and he was holding up a glass of 18-year-old Glenlivet, his favorite scotch, and proposing a toast. He remembered feeling faint when he stood up and then a sharp, stabbing pain in the side of his head. But given that his friends could often be a pain in the ass—or head, depending on the circumstances—that wasn't unusual.

Jake tried to sit up again, but at that very moment, the nurse returned with a paper cup. She was accompanied by a smiling young doctor with a stethoscope around his neck, just like on TV. Jake did his best to grab the cup, but she held it out of reach as the doctor stepped to the side of the bed.

"Mr. Silver, I'm Dr. Jordan, and I'm happy to see that you're back with the living." A wry smile played across his clean-shaven baby face.

Jake shook his head as though his ears were blocked. "Atwat?" He pointed to the cup in the nurse's hand. *Damn it! Don't they know I need some goddamn water?*

Dr. Jordan ignored him and took a metal instrument from the pocket of his lab coat. He looked into Jake's eyes and nodded. He then applied his stethoscope to several places that really should have been left alone, as far as Jake was concerned. The doctor stepped back, his smile still firmly in place. "Can you tell me your name?"

"Ja...uh...Jake. Si...Sil...ver."

Dr. Jordan's smile widened. "Excellent, excellent. What is your fiancée's name?"

That was easy. "Beth. Beth Ann."

"Wonderful! What else can you remember?"

Jake searched his mind in vain. He looked beseechingly at the doctor and the nurse, who both smiled encouragingly. Then he suddenly brightened. "Pack...uh...ers. Packers!"

Dr. Jordan frowned. "Did you say Packers?"

Jake nodded vigorously. "Packers!" he repeated.

"Do you mean the Green Bay Packers?" The doctor leaned forward.

Jake smiled broadly and did his best to give a thumbs-up.

"Oh, for God's sake, we're all Vikings fans around here." Dr. Jordan winked at the nurse. "Whaddya think, Nurse Gunderson? Maybe we should just put him out of his misery!"

"Leave him alone. I'm a Packers fan too!" The nurse laughed and handed Jake the cup of now-melting ice.

▲ ▼ ▲

That night was horrific. In addition to the stern but kind Nurse Gunderson, Jake was also under the care of the evil night shift minion, Nurse Barata. Apparently, her God-given duty was to flip on the bright fluorescent light in Jake's room every hour on the hour, just to amuse herself. At one point in the middle of the night, she'd also taken great pleasure in drawing what felt like several pints of Jake's blood. *God knows what she'll do with all my blood. Sell it on the Internet?*

He'd finally fallen back to sleep with the help of a couple Ambiens. He woke up to the sound of his door banging open and a voice asking him if he was awake. He opened his eyes to find a huge African-American man holding a tray in his immense hand. "Rise and shine, Silverado! I'm Omar, and it's time for your delicious first meal of the day," he said in a deep, sonorous voice.

Jake sat up, yawned, rubbed his eyes blearily, and gave the guy a thumbs-up.

Omar adjusted the tray table so it was on Jake's lap. "If you're wondering why I called you Silverado, it's because I always give my patients nicknames. Since you can't say much, I cut you some slack and picked the obvious one."

Jake nodded and examined the contents of the tray. There was a plastic container of sugar-free orange juice, a bowl of what appeared to be runny oatmeal, a small container of skim milk, and a plate with a slice of orange and a stick of celery. Jake yawned again, pointed to the celery, and shook his head. Omar grinned, picked up the stalk, and chomped on it. "Yeah, I know. Somebody in the kitchen ordered too much celery and figured what the hell, why not serve it for breakfast?"

Just then Jake's fiancée Beth appeared in the doorway. Omar quickly shoved the rest of the celery into his mouth, nearly choking, and it was Jake's turn to laugh. "Serves you right," Jake said clearly.

Omar stopped. "What did you say?"

"I said, it serves you right!"

Omar turned and hurried out the door. "Hey, Mr. Silver is talking and making sense!" he shouted, his voice echoing down the hall.

Beth Ann sat down on the edge of Jake's bed. "What's the big deal? You've always been able to talk, right?"

Jake removed the lid of the orange juice. "Absolutely." He took a big swallow, grimaced, and spat it back into the plastic container. "My God, that's awful!"

Omar returned with another nurse. "Silverado, I'd like you to meet Nurse Fleck. Say something to her. Tell her it serves me right for eating your celery."

Jake winked at Beth Ann. "Sllar ick rrr twerb."

Omar shook his head. "No way, man. I heard you say, 'Serves you right,' as clear as day just a couple of minutes ago. I swear it!"

Nurse Fleck scowled at Jake, spun on her heels, and left in a huff. Jake grinned at Omar. "You're damn right. It does serve you right, stealing my breakfast celery! Now how about getting me some more of that nice fresh celery with a big cup of peanut butter, and I won't report you."

Omar was speechless for a moment, and then gave a bellowing laugh. "Okay, Silverado. Now, that's funny. By

God, you had me going. I'll get you all the damn celery and peanut butter you want."

Dr. Jordan and Nurse Gunderson walked into the room. Nurse Gunderson, who was dressed in scrubs covered with Minnesota Twins logos, put her hand on Jake's shoulder. "Good morning, Mr. Silver. And what do you have to say for yourself this morning?"

Jake looked around at his audience. "Get. Me. The. Hell. Out. Of. Here!" he said, carefully enunciating each word.

▲ ▼ ▲

Unfortunately for Jake, the hospital had a long list of pesky procedures, so Nurse Gunderson couldn't tell him when he was being released, only that it probably would be way ahead of the normal schedule. In the meantime, Jake was blessed—or not—by the arrival of a roommate. Jake guessed the man had also suffered a stroke, but compared to Jake, he was in seriously rough shape. To make matters worse, he'd been moaning nonstop since he arrived. In the last hour, he'd added a hacking cough to his litany, making it impossible for Jake to sleep.

When Nurse Fleck arrived at bedtime, Jake asked to be transferred to another room, but she informed him that all the other rooms were spoken for. She mentioned that he might be released after breakfast the next morning, so he texted Beth Ann and told her to pick him up at 10 a.m. He swallowed two Ambiens with a cup of water and tried to fall asleep.

At midnight, Jake was still wide awake, staring at the ceiling. He closed his eyes, crossed himself, and said a prayer. Then he pointed toward his roommate and whispered, "Just die." Before he could open his eyes, a nurse rushed into the room. She flipped on the light and pushed a blue button on the wall. In her hurry, she didn't close the curtain that separated Jake's bed from his roommate's.

"Are you okay? Can you hear me?" the nurse said urgently. The man didn't respond, so she began administering CPR. A female doctor and two nurses came into the room. The doctor murmured something to the nurses, and one of them quickly injected the contents of a syringe into the man's arm while the other nurse began setting up a drip. A burly man wearing gray scrubs pushed a red crash cart with a defibrillator into the room. The doctor instructed the first nurse to charge the defibrillator while he gripped the paddles. Less than five seconds later, she gave the all-clear order and applied the paddles to the man's chest. Jake could see that the lines on the monitor remained flat. The doctor applied the paddles two more times, but there was no response.

The doctor replaced the paddles and instructed the nurses to remove the machine from the room. She sat on the edge of the man's bed and bowed her head. Clearly, the man was dead, and nothing was going to bring him back. Stunned, Jake rolled over and looked out the window. *Did I just make that guy die?*

▲ ▼ ▲

The next morning, Omar arrived with a breakfast tray and an extra plate of celery and peanut butter, followed by Beth Ann carrying Jake's duffel bag. At 10 a.m., Nurse Gunderson showed up, only to inform them that she was still waiting for Dr. Jordan to sign Jake's discharge papers. Jake grumbled, but Beth Ann fluffed his pillows and settled herself in an armchair. She picked up the remote and turned the channel to CNN, even though Jake usually watched Fox News, and not just because the talking heads were attractive blondes. The TV was on mute, and they watched a private plane carrying Kim Jong-un, the leader of North Korea, land at a Chinese airport.

Jake scowled. He was just about to flip the bird at the TV, but something made him stop. He flashed back to his childhood, when flipping the bird was nearly as bad as taking the Lord's name in vain. He was 16, and he'd just passed his driver's test in his mother's car, with her in the passenger seat. Another driver cut him off, and Jake raised his hand to give him the finger. "Jacob! What on earth are you thinking?" his mother cried. She leaned over and caught his hand in hers. "You must never, ever give anyone the finger, especially when they're driving. Who knows? That driver might be an escaped convict or have a gun with him—or both!" Jake blushed and slowed down to add some distance between them and the errant driver. His mother sat back and said, "Now, it's okay to be annoyed, but instead of showing your irritation, just point discreetly at the person and say the words, 'Just die.'"

So, instead of giving Kim Jong-un the finger, Jake pointed his finger at the TV and whispered, "Just die." At that very moment, Nurse Gunderson walked into the room, waving Jake's papers. Jake threw aside the covers and tried to get out of bed, but she pushed him back against the pillows.

"Take it easy, fella. I need to go over these instructions with you and your fiancée." Beth Ann was listening intently, but Jake was staring at the TV screen. Kim Jong-un was lying motionless on the tarmac, and the closed captions declared he'd fainted. Chaos ensued as the North Korean handlers pushed away the Chinese aides, and the news feed was quickly replaced with another topic.

Nurse Gunderson handed Jake a piece of paper and a pen. He scribbled his signature and gave it back to her. She laughed and said, "You are now a free man. Here, let's get you out of here." She and Beth Ann helped Jake into the wheelchair. Beth Ann hooked his duffel bag to the handles, carefully wheeled him down the hall to the elevator, navigated the wheelchair inside, and pressed the button for the main floor.

A young man in a valet jacket pushed Jake's wheelchair out to the curb where the Beth Ann's car was waiting. Jake tried to stand up but lost his balance, so the valet steadied him and helped him into the passenger seat. The valet was grinning. He said, "Hey, did you hear that Kim Jong-un died in China ten minutes ago?"

Jake leaned back against the seat and closed his eyes. *This is too weird. Did I just kill the leader of North Korea?*

▲ ▼ ▲

Beth Ann drove out of the parking lot and nearly collided with a bright purple convertible Corvette when the driver took a sharp left turn into the lot. The driver gave Beth Ann the finger, and she was just about to return the favor when Jake reached over and covered her hand with his. "Haven't I ever told you what my mom thinks about flipping the bird?"

"Tell me later. Right now, I just want to get you home."

"Okay, me too. Thanks for being my personal chauffeur and nurse. I'm sorry you had to wait so long this morning."

"Oh, sweetheart, it's not your fault. I just don't know why Dr. Jordan couldn't have signed your papers earlier. It just feels like doctors have no respect for other people's time."

"Yikes. Those are pretty strong words for a soon-to-be veterinarian."

"Well, they don't! It seems like the entire hospital revolves around the doctors, and everyone else is just there to do their goddamn bidding. As you just experienced, most of the caregiving is provided by the nurses and the hospital staff, yet the doctors get all the glory and the big paychecks."

Jake shook his head. "That may be true, but I'm grateful to Dr. Jordan—and you. He said the real reason I'm alive is that you recognized I was having a stroke. If you hadn't gotten me to the hospital within three hours, I'd be in much rougher shape, and you'd be feeding me with a straw for the rest of my life."

"Yes, that's probably true. But let's not forget the researchers. You're fortunate to be the recipient of that next-gen tissue plasminogen activator drug, which is a big part of the reason you're still here."

She turned into the driveway of Jake's home. It was a spacious modern rambler with a walkout basement and a wraparound deck that overlooked a bike trail. She touched the garage door opener and pulled into the stall where Jake's fleet of bicycles were hanging on the wall. Jake loved biking to Lake Calhoun in Minneapolis, an easy, 20-mile jaunt.

Jake looked at the bikes. *Can't drive a car, but Nurse Gunderson never told me I couldn't ride my bikes.*

Beth Ann put the car in park and touched Jake's knee. "You just sit right there, and I'll come around and help you get out."

Jake shook his head. "I'm fine!" He opened the door and eased his six-foot-plus frame out of the car. He caught his reflection in the rearview mirror and grimaced. His dark, wavy hair was matted, and his skin was the color of frozen walleye. Fortunately, he still had his signature Kirk Douglas dimple in the middle of his chin. He stretched, sniffed his armpit, recoiled, and lost his balance. "Whoa!" He grabbed the car to steady himself.

"Goddamn it, Jake!" Beth Ann cried. "What part of staying put didn't you understand?"

2

OMAR CARTER PUNCHED OUT ON the time clock in the bowels of Abbott Northwestern Hospital. He opened his locker, stuffed his old leather blackjack into the back of his pants, pulled his shirt down over his hips, and walked up the steps to the exit. He pushed open the heavy door, looked up at the late August sun, and grinned. Summer in Minnesota was fleeting at best, and he wanted to get back to his tiny apartment and go for a run around Lake Calhoun.

Abbott was one of the premier hospitals in the state, yet, ironically, it was located in one of the riskier neighborhoods. Even Omar, as big as he was, didn't feel comfortable in this part of town, which is why he carried the blackjack. His meager 15-dollar-an-hour wage was not enough to cover the high cost of the hospital parking lot, so his old Camry was five blocks away.

Unbeknownst to most of his colleagues, Omar had once been a Green Bay Packer. Ten years ago, he was one of the best defensive ends in pro football. He'd set the league on fire, making the Pro Bowl every year. But a chop block from a rookie Oakland Raider had left him limping, which took him out of the NFL. Then his divorce from a gold-digging Dallas Cowboys cheerleader took darn near everything he owned, except for his beloved Super Bowl ring and a long-term real estate investment.

At that point, his life quickly spiraled out of control. He started drinking and spending money profligately until one morning, when he woke up hung over without a dollar in his wallet and a bunch of maxed-out credit cards. He called his financial manager and asked if he could cash in on his investment, but the guy said no dice, not yet.

So Omar, too proud to hang around Green Bay dead broke, got into his Camry and headed to Minneapolis, a larger city where he could easily disappear. And for the most part, he was right. With his Super Bowl ring stashed in a drawer, he'd found the job at Abbott. Every morning, he delivered breakfast to the patients while daydreaming about the day he could finally quit his menial job.

▲ ▼ ▲

Omar approached his car and saw four men sitting on the hood. The fact that they were black was not surprising, since the neighborhood was home to immigrants from all over the world. What did surprise Omar was that they'd picked his rusty, 12-year-old Camry to use as a sofa. Omar reached behind him and made sure the blackjack was in place. He took several steps forward and then said, "Hey, brothers, thanks for keeping an eye on my ride. I appreciate it."

One of the men stepped away from the sedan, a hostile half-smile on his face and sleeve tattoos snaking around each arm. Omar looked straight at him and said, "Hey, bro, what's happening?" but just nodded at the other guys, making eye contact with each of them and taking their measure. One was clearly a teenager. Despite the August heat, the kid was wearing a jacket, so Omar figured he was carrying a handgun. The punk on his left was nearly as big as Omar, yet he was pretty much all fat. He couldn't have been more than 17, but he already had a double chin. The guy on Omar's right was as rail-thin as a New York model, his face ravaged by acne, with a giant herpes blister on his upper lip. He was older than his counterparts, so Omar clocked him as the leader.

"I'll tell you what's happening, bro. You are parking on our turf," the guy said with a nasty snicker. "And that needs to be accounted for."

"Did you really just say, 'it needs to be accounted for?'"

The man glanced at his buddies.

"That's an impressive sentence structure for a street punk," Omar said calmly.

The man puckered his lips and tilted his tattooed skull toward Omar. "Who you calling a punk?"

Omar pointed at the youngest guy. "How about him?"

The leader turned to look at the teen and Omar planted his good leg and bull-rushed the boy as if he were a quarterback who needed to be taken out of the game. Realizing what was happening, the leader turned and pulled a Bowie knife from behind his back. Omar's NFL instincts kicked in, and he slammed the guy into the hood of the Camry. The guy tried to sit up, but Omar delivered a vicious headbutt. His eyes rolled up and back into his head, and he fell off the car, his knife dropping to the ground.

The fat guy moved toward Omar, surprising him with his agility. He tried to emulate Omar's rush and headbutt, but Omar whipped out the blackjack and walloped him on the side of his head. At that moment, the leader took a flying leap and landed on Omar's back. Omar spun around and sent him sailing. The guy landed in the street and stood up, waving Omar's wallet in the air before running into an alley.

Omar turned to the last man. He had a vicious smile on his scarred face and was holding a SIG Sauer P938 handgun in a drug addict's shaky grip. The Bowie knife lay at Omar's feet, and he bent down to pick it up. *Oh, shit, bringing a knife to a gun fight. Not good.*

Omar flipped the knife over and grabbed it by the flat side of the shaft. Taking aim, he hurled it at the chubby guy's tattooed head and watched the guy fall to the ground. The SIG dropped out of his hand and bounced toward Omar. Omar jumped over, kicked the gun under his car, and hefted his blackjack.

Meanwhile, the guy was staggering to his feet. He shook his head to clear the cobwebs and looked around for the gun. Not finding it, he grabbed the knife instead and turned to face Omar, who was hiding his blackjack behind his right hip. The guy grinned and swished the knife in front of himself as if he were in a Shakespearean fencing duel. After a few seconds, he jabbed it at Omar's chest.

He had no way of knowing that Omar had been one of the NFL's most fearsome pass rushers, famous for his swim move, bull rush, and an *olé* move that would have made any matador proud. The swim move seemed to Omar to be the most appropriate in this circumstance, so he deftly spun around the fat teen. He solidly backhanded the guy with his blackjack, catching him on the skull just above the neck. The guy dropped to the ground like a puppet with his strings cut, just as a Minneapolis squad car pulled up, its rack flashing red and blue. The doors opened and two cops stepped out, their revolvers drawn.

"Put the gun down and put your hands in the air!" one of the cops thundered.

Omar paused and looked around, wondering who the officer was addressing.

"Do it now!" the cop shouted, and Omar realized his blackjack had been mistaken for a gun. He dropped it immediately and thrust his well-muscled arms into the blue August sky.

"Don't shoot! For God's sake, don't shoot!" Omar pleaded.

.

3

BETH ANN REACHED FOR JAKE'S arm and helped him regain his balance. They walked slowly into the house and paused in the mudroom so he could catch his breath. When they got to the kitchen, she helped him sit in his favorite chair and sat down across from him.

"Thanks again for all your help, Beth Ann. I love you big tons."

"And I love you, even if you are a horse's patootie. It's good to have you back, stubbornness and all. You had me scared."

"I was also scared. I owe you my life."

"Well, if we're keeping score, I guess I did kind of save your life. Now how about if we sit on the deck and watch the Twins game?"

"Excellent! How about I mix us up a couple of Cosmos and order a pizza?"

"Goddamn it, Jake!" Beth Ann reached over and softly backhanded him. "Don't you even think about alcohol. You just had a freakin' stroke. But now that you mention it, a deep-dish pizza from Detello's would be marvelous."

"Great! I'll order it." He called the restaurant and ordered a house special with extra sauce. "It'll be ready in 20 minutes, so I'll go pick it up."

"Oh, no, not on your life! You just sit right here and I'll go get it. And no drinking while I'm gone."

Jake picked up the remote and flicked on the TV. He caught another whiff of his BO *Cripes, I stink!* He walked slowly to the master bathroom, holding on to the wall for balance. He dropped his clothes in a heap on the floor and turned on the hot water. He took his time, reveling in the feeling of being home. He toweled himself off and looked in the mirror, turning his head from side to side and admiring the stubble. *Maybe I should grow a beard?* But he rejected the idea and picked up his razor.

When he was finished, he fingered the small, C-shaped scar that ran from his left temple almost to his left eye and shuddered at the memory it evoked.

When Jake was about 12, playing hide-and-seek at Bill O'Neil's house, he ducked into a large woodpile. It was getting dark, so he didn't see the old board with a rusty nail sticking out. When his temple connected with the nail, he recoiled, dragging the nail through his skin. Blood pouring down his face, he pulled off his T-shirt, wadded it into a bundle, and pressed it to the wound.

He ran home, barely able to see, and stumbled through the back door. His mother took one look at him and guided him to the sink, where she washed the cut and applied orange Mercurochrome. She crisscrossed two Band-Aids over the wound and pronounced him fit for battle again. The cut healed quickly, but left a long scar.

When Jake was very tired or under stress, his eyelid would droop, which it was doing right now. He stared at his reflection. On a good day, he looked like Cary Grant, with his indigo eyes, and Kirk Douglas, with his trademark dimple. Today, not so much. He put on a pair of sweats and went back to the kitchen. Beth Ann was back from Detello's. As she opened the pizza box, and the smell of garlic was intoxicating. He took two cans of Diet Coke from the fridge and filled their glasses with ice. Beth Ann carried the plates out to the deck, and Jake followed her with the drinks.

They devoured the pizza in a matter of minutes as they watched the pre-game. The Twins were leading their division, which amazed Jake and every other Twins fan. Before this season, the club had been so bad for so long that nobody could believe they now had the best record in baseball.

Beth Ann finished the last bite of pizza and sighed contentedly. She looked over the deck at a bicyclist on the path below. He was dressed in dark clothes with a hoodie pulled over his head, and he was yelling loudly into his cell phone. He was obviously not happy with the person on the other end, as his tirade was full of f-bombs and other expletives. Beth Ann got up from her chair and leaned over the railing. "Hey, knock it off!" she yelled. "There are young children in this neighborhood!"

The man looked up and gave Beth Ann the finger. "Go to hell!" he screamed and began pedaling away.

Beth Ann sat down, her hands shaking. "What a jerk! What's that phrase your mom taught you to say?"

"You point your finger at the person and say, 'Just die.' Like this." Jake stood up, pointed at the bicyclist, and said the words. At that very moment, the young man veered off the path and collided with an enormous oak tree. Jake's heart pounded as he stared at the guy lying in a heap on the ground. "Oh, my God, Beth Ann, let's get down there."

4

THE COPS MOVED SLOWLY TOWARD Omar. He dropped the blackjack as if it were a hot potato and raised his hands. One of the officers picked it up and examined it. "So you weren't packing heat?"

"No, sir, just my trusty old blackjack," Omar replied quietly.

The second cop moved toward the gang while the first cop slid his Glock 45 back into its holster and slapped the blackjack into his palm. "Now this brings back old memories."

"Yes, sir, it served its purpose, especially when those four nitwits attacked me."

The cop glanced over at his partner, who was handcuffing the young men. "Nice job, but you know blackjacks are illegal in Minnesota."

"Um, no, not if you have a permit," Omar replied.

"Yeah, that's right, so drop your hands and show me your permit."

Omar reached for the wallet in his back pocket, but quickly realized he'd been pick-pocketed by one of the gang. "Aw, shoot, one of the bangers took my wallet off me."

"Yeah, right." The cop frowned and pointed at the Camry. "Assume the position, which I'm sure you've done before."

Omar leaned against the car, his hands and feet spread wide, and sighed deeply. The cop was right. It was nearly impossible to be a large black man and not have been in this situation.

"Well, if you don't have a permit, then you get to spend the night in jail until we get this all sorted out," the cop said.

"Man, I got to go to work in the morning. I'm on probation already. If I skip a day, they'll fire my black ass."

"Sorry, man, just following procedure." He handcuffed Omar, patted him down, and ushered him into the back seat of the squad car. Omar watched through the window as the other cop handcuffed the gang members, pushed them into a white police van, and slammed the door

▲ ▼ ▲

Jake and Beth Ann ran down to the trail. "Be careful, the grass is wet," Jake said. At that very moment, Beth Ann, who was behind him, slipped, and her cell phone went flying. Jake caught the movement out of the corner of his eye and turned back to help her, all thoughts of the biker gone from his mind.

"Son of a bitch, Beth Ann, are you okay?"

"No, goddamn it. I'm not okay," she moaned. She tried to stand up, but her left ankle buckled, and she fell back to the ground. Thankfully, she was only 110 pounds soaking wet, so Jake cradled her in his arms. Ignoring her protestations, he carried her back to the house and settled her in an armchair with an ice pack.

"Thank you, Jake, for saving me instead of the asshole cyclist. I wonder what happened to him." Just then, they heard an ambulance siren outside the house. Jake watched two paramedics making their way down the hill to the tree, where the bicyclist was lying motionless.

"Yikes, I wonder if he's dead," Jake said.

"Oh, my God. What if your mom's curse really works?"

"Now that's a scary thought, so let's change the subject. How's your ankle feeling?"

"Not good. I think I should go to the hospital and have it checked. But you're not going with me. You've had enough excitement in the last few days."

Jake opened his mouth to disagree, but Beth Ann shot him a warning look. "And don't fight me on this one. I should never have let you carry me up from the backyard. What a stupid stunt. You could've had another stroke, and you might not have been so goddamn lucky a second time."

"Well, you need to get to the emergency room, and you certainly can't drive."

"Oh, nonsense, it's my left ankle, not my right, so I can drive just fine. But I am worried about leaving you here all alone, my love."

"Fine, then I'll drive you to the hospital."

"Goddamn it, Jake, you're not allowed to drive."

"Then it looks like I'm staying here!"

"You win. Just stay out of the scotch and go to bed early."

Beth Ann drove herself to the hospital, promising to call as soon as she had any news. Jake decided to call it a day. He set a bottle of water on the nightstand, closed the shades, cranked the Bose white noise machine, and flipped on the overhead fan. He slid under the covers and thought about the bicyclist. *Did I cause the accident by saying the words, 'Just die'? Should I tell my mother, since it was her idea?*

Jake decided against telling his mother, even though she'd always been supportive of him and his adventures. Maybe he'd tell his dad, Arnie. He smiled as he thought of his father, who was a successful corporate attorney at Sentry Insurance in Stevens Point, Wisconsin. Jake thought back to his childhood in Park Ridge, a tiny village on the outskirts of Stevens Point. His father served as the treasurer of the village board, so he was in charge of giving out bicycle licenses. When Jake got his first real bike, his dad gave him the coveted #1 license plate. Jake knew it was his dad's way of doing something special for him, since he worked an awful lot and rarely got to see Jake's baseball and basketball games. Jake remembered how jealous his buddies were, especially Hank Mutter, one of his best friends. Jake and Hank had stayed in touch, albeit off and on, and he was going to be best man at Jake and Beth Ann's wedding.

Arnie had imparted to his son his love of reading, especially James Bond books, and Bond movies, as well. Jake smiled at the memory and then grimaced. As a teenager, he never understood that Bond's behaviors, which he eagerly emulated, were those of a quintessential narcissist.

As a result, Jake's attitude toward women was egotistical. He dated only sporadically, usually catching a woman on the rebound from an unsuccessful relationship. He'd met Beth Ann under such circumstances at a Twins game sponsored by his broker. He'd been seated next to her, who was with a young financial planner who was drinking heavily. As Beth Ann's date became increasingly inebriated, he started swearing loudly at the opposing team until Twins security removed him from the stadium, leaving Beth Ann high and dry—at which point Jake introduced himself.

After they had been dating for three years, Jake finally popped the question. Beth Ann accepted immediately, with one caveat—she wasn't getting married until she was Dr. Beth Ann Noble, DVM, and had a full-time job in a veterinary clinic.

Jake checked his phone. No word yet from her yet, so he allowed himself to doze off.

Two hours later, he woke up to a phone call from Beth Ann. She happily informed him that her ankle was only sprained, not broken, so she was on her way home. He sat up in bed, turned on the light, and sipped from a bottle of water. His cell phone chirped once more. Thinking it was Beth Ann again, he picked it up from his nightstand. It was an unknown number.

5

WHEN THE POLICE CAR PULLED UP outside the station, the cop in the passenger seat turned around to address Omar. "Your home, sweet home, at least for tonight." He pointed to the Super Bowl ring on Omar's finger. "Where'd you steal that pricey gem?"

"Nah, it's just a knockoff, 49 bucks on Amazon."

"Huh. Maybe my buddy and I should get a couple so we can impress the ladies."

Both cops laughed. The first cop opened Omar's door and pointed the way into the station. Just as Omar knew would happen, he was given the royal treatment. He was fingerprinted, photographed, tested for alcohol, and assigned to a foul-smelling holding cell. He sat down on the cot and put his head in his hands. *Gosh darn it. Why the heck am I so unlucky?* He sighed and lay back on the rock-hard mattress, doing his best to straighten his game leg. *On the other hand, I still have my ring.*

Omar spent a restless night, dispirited and disgusted. Being in jail was unwarranted since he did have a permit for the blackjack. But he'd learned a hard lesson when he acquired the leather weapon in his hometown of Milwaukee. Try as he might, he'd never been able to lose the memory that proved how devastating the blackjack could be.

Omar had grown up in a not-so-wonderful section of Milwaukee with his adoptive parents, Tom and Mary Jane Michaud. The Michauds were both whiter than snow, living among neighbors darker than midnight. He and Mary Jane adopted Omar when he was ten years old, after Omar's birth mother was found dead of an overdose. He was an only child, with no father, and no one else wanted to take him in, since he looked like he could eat a horse at one sitting and come away hungry. But Tom and Mary Jane were happy to feed Omar, and they pulled him off the streets and into the church where Tom was the minister.

Early on, the Michauds discovered that beneath all that bravado, Omar was intelligent and shrewd, with a sparkling personality and a gift for storytelling. Under the Michauds' loving care, Omar did very well in his new Christian school, where Tom also served as the assistant football coach, team chaplain, and leader of team prayers.

Omar took to football like a duck to water. He excelled at both offense and defense and quickly became the star of the team, leading them to a state title in the tiny Christian league. Though he was shy around girls, Omar was a loyal friend and became one of the most popular students in the small high school. Given his size, his friends quickly learned Omar was a good man to have on one's side in a fight.

One afternoon, Omar and his best friend Zeke were headed to the A&W root beer stand with fistfuls of dollar bills from washing all the windows in the church, including the stained-glass panes. Zeke was the third string running back of the football team. His real name was Zen Chin, and he was originally from Singapore. He was small, just over five feet, but as strong as a bull, with not one iota of backup in him.

On the way to the A&W, Omar and Zeke ran into three young black punks. They looked to be in their twenties, and while they were nowhere as big as Omar, one had a knife and another had a blackjack. The leader pointed at Zeke's new shoes and smirked. "Hey, Nip, you're wearing my shoes. Hand them over."

Zeke took a step forward. "Nip? For Chrissakes, I'm not Japanese, I'm Chinese. And as to my shoes, I think I'll keep them." He spun on his left foot and smashed his right foot into the punk's kneecap, letting out a yell that would make any Confederate rebel proud. The gang member screamed in agony as he fell to the ground, grabbing his damaged knee. Wasting no time, Zeke thrust his left foot into the shoulder of the punk wielding the knife. Zeke kicked him a second time and the knife went flying, sending the guy scurrying away in search of his weapon.

In the meantime, Omar was dealing with the owner of the blackjack. As Omar moved toward him with a bull rush, he felt a solid blow from the blackjack on his left forearm. Despite the searing pain, Omar headbutted the guy, and he dropped to the cracked sidewalk without making a sound, just as a black-and-white police car pulled up with its lights flashing: red . . . blue . . . red . . . blue . . .

Two officers, one Asian and one African-American, emerged from the squad. "Hey, Zen, how's the hammer hanging?" the Asian officer said as he surveyed the carnage.

"Hey, Fang, it's hanging just fine!" Zeke replied. "Where the hell have you been? You're like a blister—you show up when the work is done."

"Well, it looks like you did okay for yourself. Who's your big buddy?"

Zeke looked at Omar, who was holding his forearm and grimacing in pain. "This is my friend Omar Carter. You've heard of him—he's the star of our football team. Omar, meet Weng Fang." Omar and Fang nodded at each other.

The African-American cop was handcuffing the punks and leading them away to the squad car. "Looks like you took a shot from that blackjack," Officer Fang said to Omar, pointing to the leather sap on the ground.

"Yeah, it hurts like hell. I think he might have broken my arm."

The police officer shook his head. "Probably not, but you're going to have one hell of a bruise." He pointed to the blackjack. "Why don't you keep that? Hell, you deserve it, but make sure you get it licensed, as it may come in handy sometime."

"Thanks, I will." Omar beamed and picked up the blackjack.

Zeke picked up the knife and winked at Officer Fang. "Hey, how about if I keep this too?"

"Well, I really shouldn't do this, but go ahead and get out of here."

Zeke grinned, stuck the blade in his pocket, and started toward the A&W.

Omar nodded his thanks to the officer and caught up with Zeke. "Hey, that cop was really a nice guy. He didn't have to do that," he said.

Zeke laughed. "Oh, yes, he did. He's my uncle."

▲ ▼ ▲

The next morning, after an unpleasant jail breakfast, Omar was loaded into a filthy police van emblazoned with the name Black Maria. He found himself next to a man who stank to high heaven. Highly articulate, he insisted on engaging Omar in conversation about life on the street. When he noticed Omar's ring, he said, "Holy smokes, it's Omar Carter!"

Omar curled his fingers into a ball and fist-bumped the man.

"Hey, man, I'm a big fan," the guy said. "What the hell are you doing here? Is this some sort of a police ride-along?"

For the first time in 24 hours, Omar laughed out loud. "Yup, absolutely! I get a tour of the courthouse and, if I'm lucky, I get to meet a real judge and get his autograph."

The man smiled. "Well, then, how about an autograph from you?"

"Sure, got a pen?"

"Naw, I don't have a pen, gosh darn it." The man's face fell. The van stopped and an officer opened the back door and ushered Omar and his companion out. He led them through a door that connected to the courtroom.

Omar's case was the second of the day. The judge looked down at him, first with a scowl, then a grin. "Omar Carter, as I live and breathe. What the heck are you doing in my courtroom?"

"I don't really know, your honor. I guess I was in the wrong place at the wrong time." He then explained everything that had happened the day before, leaving out the fact that a SIG Sauer had been kicked under his car.

The judge listened intently and looked at the arresting officer, who was sitting in the back row with the other cops, most of whom were napping. "Officer Williamson, Officer Peter Williamson?" the judge called out.

One of the officers stood up groggily. "Here, sir, I mean, Your Honor."

"Officer Williamson, do you have any idea who you arrested?"

"Ah, no sir, uh, Your Honor," the officer said meekly.

The judge shook his head in disgust. "This man was the most feared NFL defensive tackle of his time. Even when they would double or triple team him, he'd still get to the quarterback. This is no less than Mr. Omar Carter, a first-round draft out of the University of Tennessee. Go, Rocky Top! This man is one of the greatest Green Bay Packers to ever put on a uniform, and you, Officer Williamson, are not worthy of carrying his jockstrap."

The officer jerked his head back as though someone had drilled a football at his face. His mouth dropped open. "Umm, well, gee, Your Honor, he had an illegal blackjack in his possession."

The judge looked down at Omar and back at the officer. "It says here that Mr. Carter has a permit for it."

"Well, yes, that's what he said, but he also claimed one of the gangbangers ripped off his wallet, so he didn't have the permit on him."

"So, did you check the computer? Does he, or does he not, have a permit?"

"Ah, no, Your Honor, I didn't check," Officer Williamson replied. He stared at his shoes and muttered something about it not being his job.

"Well, a simple computer check would have confirmed Mr. Carter's permit. At the very least, you could have made a call to the dispatcher, and he could have checked on it before you made the arrest. Why the hell don't you cops think outside the box once in a while?"

The officer continued to stare silently at his shoes. The judge slammed down his gavel, causing the dozing officers in the back row to jolt awake. "Damn it. Case dismissed, and I really apologize for this, Mr. Carter."

Omar stood up and grinned at the judge. "Am I free to go? I'm really late for my job."

"Absolutely, but before you go, how about an autograph for my son? He's a big fan of yours."

6

OMAR FINALLY ESCAPED THE courtroom after signing more than a dozen autographs, including one for the cop who'd arrested him. He walked out into the summer heat and looked up at the sky. A foggy, rust-colored haze enveloped the city, likely from Canadian wildfires. He had no wallet, no money, and no ride to his Camry. A black-and-white taxi rolled by. He briefly thought about hailing it and paying the driver with an autograph, but an idea stuck in his craw. *Damn. Where did that guy live? Victoria?* He pulled out his phone and googled Jacob Silver, Victoria, then dialed the number. After three or four rings, a guy answered.

"This is Jake Silver."

Omar nearly hung up, but then decided what the hell. "Hey, Silverado, it's Omar!"

"Omar?"

"Omar from the hospital. You remember me?"

"Oh, hey, Omar, of course I do. How come you're checking up on me? Is this some kind of special hospital service?"

"Um, no, not really, but I'm kind of jammed up, and I don't really know too many people here. I thought maybe you could come pick me up."

"Uh, Omar, I don't know what to say. You remember I had a stroke, right?"

"I sure do. I might be jammed up, but I haven't forgotten the tough shape you were in. But can I tell you what happened? Then if you don't want to help me, you can say no."

Jake leaned back against the pillows, thinking of how much he'd enjoyed seeing Omar every morning. "Sure, Omar, go ahead. I'm all ears."

Omar took a breath and launched into his story, sparing no detail about getting mugged, doing a swim move, and spending a night in jail.

Jake listened intently. "Omar, did you say swim move?"

"Yeah, I was even kind of famous for it."

Jake laughed. "You mean like swimming in a pool?"

Now it was Omar's turn to laugh. "Oh, for God's sake, Silverado, not in a pool, in the NFL! I was a defensive end for the Packers. As you may remember, we won the Super Bowl."

Jake sat upright in his bed. "Omar, are you Omar Carter, future NFL Hall of Famer?"

Omar laughed even harder. "Well, I don't know about the Hall of Fame, but I do have the ring."

"Seriously, Omar? I had no idea. What the hell are you doing delivering meals to mere mortals at the hospital?"

Omar sighed. "It's a long story. But if you'll come and pick me up and give me a ride to the hospital, I'll tell you everything."

"Wait, are you expecting me to pick you up in a car?"

"Yes! Didn't you hear what I said before? I have no wallet, no ride, and I'm stuck out in front of this damn cop shop."

"Omar, you know I can't drive without a doctor's release."

"Oh, that's bullshit. They didn't take your driver's license away from you, did they?"

"Um, no, they didn't."

"Well, then, you can still drive. They just tell people that to limit their liability."

"I don't know. Are you sure?"

"Yes, I'm sure, Silverado. You'll be fine."

Jake thought for a moment. "All right. For a Packer, I'll do it!"

"Aw, that's great, Jake. I really appreciate it."

"So where exactly are you? Which cop shop?"

Omar looked behind him at the monstrosity of a building. "Well, I think it's the main one in downtown Minneapolis. I can tell you it's the ugliest cop shop I've ever seen. The color reminds me of puke."

Jake laughed. "Yeah, that's the Minneapolis courthouse. You're right, it does look like vomit, now that you mention it. Hey, by the way, are you anywhere near Edelman's Deli?"

"I'm right across the street."

"Excellent! I'm guessing you must be starving, so head over there, and I'll meet you in an hour or so."

"But I don't have any money."

"Not to worry. Just go and get whatever you want, and I'll pay when I get there."

"That'd be awesome. I am a little hungry. Listen, Jake, thanks a million." Omar hung up and put his phone in his pocket. He fell in step behind two cops who were jaywalking across the street. He held the door for them as they went into the deli and sat down at a table in the middle of the room. Omar took a booth near the door so he could make a quick exit if Jake didn't show up.

A waiter ambled slowly over to Omar and set a glass of water and a menu on the table. "Coffee?"

"Yes, please." Omar smiled at him.

"Cup or pot?" the waiter replied without returning the smile.

"Pot, with some cream."

The waiter brought the coffee and a metal jug of cream. "Are you ready to order?"

"If you're still serving breakfast, I'll have a large orange juice and five fried eggs, runny, over corned beef hash. And six, no, make that a dozen, strips of bacon, crispy. And blueberry pancakes for dessert."

"Is that all, sir?"

The addition of "sir" was not lost on Omar, who knew the waiter was calculating his rapidly expanding gratuity. Omar opened the menu and pointed to a photo of a burger. "Let's add a double cheeseburger, medium rare, hold the fries."

"Absolutely, sir. Would you like me to bring the food as it's ready, or do you want everything at the same time?"

"Go ahead and bring it as soon as it's ready. I'm starving."

The waiter smiled for the first time. "In that case, you might as well get the French fries, since they come with the cheeseburger, and they can be ready in a jiffy."

Omar grinned. "Excellent idea! And don't forget the ketchup."

The waiter pointed at a full bottle of Heinz ketchup between the salt and pepper shakers. "If that's not enough, I'll be happy to bring more."

▲ ▼ ▲

When Jake was double-checking that his front door was locked before he left for Minneapolis, he saw two men in dark suits leaving his neighbors' house and walking toward his. He quickly realized they were police. He considered opening the door for them, but since Omar was waiting, he went to the garage and got into his pale yellow 1970 Jaguar XKE. He could see that the men were talking to his other neighbor, Juliet Hanes. When she saw Jake's car, she waved, and the men turned to look at him, one with a smile and one with a frown.

Good cop, bad cop. He hit the gas pedal and accelerated out of the cul-de-sac. He wondered who the biker was and whether he'd died. Cops knocking on doors was never a good thing.

▲ ▼ ▲

Beth Ann was sitting in the last row of a large auditorium on the St. Paul campus of the University of Minnesota, a crutch propped up on the empty seat next to hers. The professor, Hillary Crane, was a tall, thin, 50-something woman with a wonderful sense of humor. She was sharp as a tack and a tough grader, but Beth Ann was leading the class with an A+. While Professor Crane explained the nuances of bovine nutrition, Beth Ann surreptitiously ate an egg salad sandwich, trying not to drop anything on her pants. As she chewed, she thought about the last few days. The fact that Jake had a stroke was disconcerting enough, but this business of just die was even more so.

Beth Ann was in love with Jake, or at least she thought she was. He was kind, handsome, fit, and an all-around good guy. Plus, he was really in love with her, which was important. Before meeting Jake, Beth Ann hadn't dated much, and she knew Jake was a good catch. Beth Ann sighed. She wished her grandmother, Gammy Lou, were still alive so she could talk to her about Jake.

Gammy Lou was Beth Ann's maternal grandmother, and she was a straight shooter. She lived on a farm in Iowa, where she and her brother Wilbur raised cattle and grew tons of corn. She only went to church on the day after Christmas "to avoid the Christmas rush," as she liked to say. "I only need to check in with the good Lord once a year because he knows damn well I'm too busy to attend every Sunday. And hell, I'm too busy to even sin, even though that'd be fun now and then."

When Beth Ann was 14, Gammy Lou invited her to live on the farm for the summer. They had four dogs, too many cats to count, and one cow, a sweet-tempered Guernsey named Daisy that Beth Ann milked every morning. Gammy Lou watched Beth Ann fall in love with animals and develop her first crush, which was on the traveling vet who regularly visited the farm. Before Gammy Lou died, she made Beth Ann the beneficiary of her modest life insurance policy so she could pursue her dream of being a veterinarian.

When her mother came to pick her up at the end of the summer, Beth Ann hid in the hayloft with a bag of Doritos, a bottle of water, and her favorite dog, a pretty white golden retriever named Sophie. The next morning, Beth Ann watched from her perch as her mother walked to her car. She opened the door, but before she got in, she cupped her hands and called to Beth Ann, her voice breaking. "I love you and I understand why you don't want to go home, so it's okay if you stay here." Her mother got into the car, wiped away a tear, and drove slowly down the long, dusty driveway.

Beth Ann waited for more than an hour, then she and Sophie climbed down from the loft and trudged wearily up the stairs into the kitchen. Gammy Lou was sitting at the kitchen table, sipping coffee. She smiled at Beth Ann and opened her arms for a hug. The young woman began sobbing. Gammy Lou held her tightly and stroked her hair.

When Beth Ann's tears subsided, Gammy spoke quietly. "I'm not sure what's going on at home, Beth Ann. Your mother didn't explain, but she alluded to the fact that there's something nasty going on with your father. You don't have to tell me anything unless you want to. But understand, I've never cared for that pompous, holier-than-thou, fire-and-brimstone-shouting, whiskey-drinking asshole of a preacher. As your mother told you, you are welcome to stay here as long as you like. Now, you must be famished, so I'll make you some breakfast, and then we have chores to do.

▲ ▼ ▲

Omar had finished his enormous meal, and the restaurant was beginning to fill up with more cops and other lunch customers. The waiter had delivered the check and returned several times, apparently hoping Omar would either pay or order more food. Omar was filled to the gills, but he finally ordered a slice of apple pie with ice cream, hoping that Jake would walk through the door. He looked around the restaurant at the sea of blue uniforms and sighed. If he had to dine and dash, he was going to be in trouble. The waiter delivered the pie, scribbled the price on Omar's check, and strode off in a huff. Omar looked at the pie and sighed again.

Just then, Jake slid into the booth. "Sorry I'm late, Mr. Carter. I really needed to take a shower, and I had to avoid a couple of policemen at my door." He reached over to shake Omar's hand, noticing his Super Bowl ring. Omar smiled and pushed the pie toward Jake.

"Not a problem, Silverado. I'm just glad you're here so I don't have to make a bum's rush. Hungry?"

Jake looked at the pie. "Why, yes, I am! I didn't have time to eat breakfast. I'd also love a cup of coffee."

Omar signaled to the waiter and held up the coffee pot. The waiter returned with a fresh pot, and Jake pulled his American Express card out of his wallet. The waiter frowned. "I'm sorry, sir, we don't take Amex."

Jake put the card back in his wallet. He pulled out a crisp fifty-dollar bill and handed it to the waiter, who shook his head and pointed to the check on the table. "That won't cover it."

Jake picked up the check and burst out laughing, causing the other patrons to look over at the unlikely pair. "Holy smoly, Omar, is there enough food left over in here for the lunch crowd?" Jake replaced the fifty with a hundred-dollar bill and handed it to the waiter. "Keep the change."

"Yes, sir, thank you sir, please take your time." He looked over at Omar with a new appreciation. "Can I get you something else, sir?"

Omar smiled and thumped his stomach. "No, I'm good."

"So, my friend, sounds like you had a rough day yesterday," Jake said through a mouthful of pie.

"Yeah, it certainly wasn't the best day of my life."

"I'm sorry about that. How can I help my favorite ex-Packer?"

"Well, the first thing is to get back to the hospital to try to save my job."

Jake took one last bite and pushed the plate away. "Well, then, let's get going."

The pair left the restaurant and drove to Jake's car, which had a ticket on the windshield. Omar pointed to the fire hydrant, and Jake groaned and grabbed the ticket. He opened the passenger door and motioned for Omar to get in the driver's side. "You're driving. I don't want to take any more chances," he said, laughing.

Omar crammed his massive body into the seat, looked down at the burl wood gear box, and grimaced. "I've never driven a stick before."

Jake rolled his eyes and sighed. "Oh, for God's sake, Omar, it's easy. Just pay attention to the clutch and the pedals, and I'll shift." Omar nodded and turned the key, then pushed in the clutch and let it out. The car jumped, nearly hitting the car parked in front of it.

"Not like that." Jake sighed again. He demonstrated the required motion, extending his hands and bringing them together again slowly. "Like two disks coming together."

Omar followed Jake's directions, gripping the leather-wrapped steering wheel as he maneuvered the Jag out of the parking place. The car jumped several times, but they made progress. "Hey, I think I've got it," Omar said.

Jake made a face. "Yeah, right. Let's try to get to the hospital in one piece, if possible."

Omar turned out to be a quick study, pulling up in front of the emergency room as if he'd handled a gear stick his entire life. He pushed his husky frame out of the car and handed the keys to Jake. "Can you wait for me?" he asked.

"Yeah, sure."

"If I'm not back in fifteen minutes, you can take off, since that means they gave me my job back."

Jake watched Omar limp through the emergency room doors and turned on the satellite radio to a classic 60s/70s rock station. The Eagles tune "Seven Bridges Road" streamed out of the Bose speakers. Jake closed his eyes and dozed in the warm sunshine. He was startled by a knock on the hood. He opened his eyes to see a meter maid holding a digital ticket device. "Sir, you need to move along. These spots are for ER patients only," she said churlishly.

"I'm sorry, but I can't, Officer. I had a stroke, and I'm not allowed to drive." He held up his wrist to show her his hospital band, thankful he'd forgotten to take it off. The meter maid shrugged and was about to issue a ticket when Omar appeared behind her.

"Hey, Thelma Louise! What's up?"

She spun around, the scowl disappearing from her face. "Hey, Omar! What are you doing here in the ER?" They fist-bumped, and Omar pointed at Jake.

"Meet my new boss, Mr. Jake Silver. I just quit my job so I can chauffeur him around in this sweet vintage ride of his."

"Nice to meet you, Mr. Silver. I'm Thelma Louise." Smiling, she canceled the ticket, took a pad of paper out of her pocket, and held it out to Omar.

"Hey, Omar, could you sign this for my nephew? He's a big Packers fan."

"Sure. What's his name?"

"Well, um, T.L. would be great." She giggled. "You could also write, 'To a wonderful person and the best Packers fan ever!'" When she saw that he'd addressed the note to Thelma Louise instead of the abbreviation, she gave him a big hug. "Aw, thanks, Omar, you've made my day!"

"And you made ours! Thanks for not giving my boss a ticket." Omar folded himself into the car, released the clutch, and drove out of the parking lot.

Jake turned to Omar. "So you quit your job?"

"Nah, my boss terminated me for not showing up yesterday. He's been looking for an excuse to get rid of me."

"Why? You're a bright spot in the patients' day."

"Well, he's got season tickets to the Vikings, and he absolutely hates the Packers and the Bears, so I guess it was inevitable."

"Well, to be honest, I hate the Bears too. My dad used to say that the only time he'd root for the Bears was if they played the Russians!"

Omar grunted his approval. "Yeah, me too. I hate the Bears and the Vikings."

"What about the Lions?"

Omar laughed, shifted the gears like a professional race car driver, and changed lanes. "Aw, Jake, you know no one gives a shit about the Lions!"

7

BETH ANN HOBBLED SLOWLY through the front door of the Krueger Veterinary Clinic, where she was an intern. There were two receptionists. The first one pushed her stylish eyeglasses higher with her middle finger and glared at Beth Ann, who returned the greeting with a half-smile. Her name was DC Krueger, and she was a millennial as well as Dr. William Krueger's daughter. DC, which was her actual given name, had three silver rings in her left nostril. Her short-sleeve shirt revealed a right arm covered with colorful tattoos, while her left bicep was emblazoned with a large pink heart with the word Daddy in the center.

Doctor Krueger, or Dr. William, as he preferred to be called, was indeed a sweetheart. While he was only an average veterinarian, he was the nicest man Beth Ann had ever met. He was also Hollywood-handsome, so everyone—women, men, and animals—immediately fell in love with him. Unfortunately, the good doctor had the worst taste in women. At the age of 58, he'd been married four times. He'd met all his wives at an upscale strip club in downtown Minneapolis, where he had a standing reservation for a corner table. DC's mom, Jennifer, a.k.a. Jasmine or Jazz, was his first. Their marriage lasted five years, just long enough for Jennifer to give birth to DC before running off with Jimbo, an ex-con who looked like George Clooney on a bad day. The next two wives had also flamed out. The fourth was about to do the same, but Dr. William didn't have a clue. He always looked bewildered when he talked about his ex-wives. He still thought that if he'd only worked harder, they wouldn't have left him. The fact that the women were all gold diggers was lost on him.

Beth Ann punched in the combination to the door that led into the back office. She looked back over her shoulder and shook her head. DC was busy filing her nails, while Darla, the other receptionist, was helping three clients all at once. Beth Ann liked Darla. She had a bubbly personality, mousy brown hair that framed a friendly, farm-girl face, and no piercings or tattoos. I guess you can't blame the customers for lining up in front of Darla.

Beth Ann limped over to her desk and settled herself in her chair. There was no one else in the office because all the vets were with clients and their pets, including dogs, cats, guinea pigs, an occasional snake and, Beth Ann's favorite, a beautiful tame wolf. She looked at the sheet of paper on her desk and groaned. It was her daily to-do list and, based on experience, she could see she'd be working late.

As the day drew to an end, she reviewed her list again, which, thankfully, had dwindled significantly. *Maybe there's still time to pick up Chipotle and see Jake tonight.* She looked up from her notes to find Dr. William standing near her desk, waiting for her to look up.

"Hello, Beth Ann. What happened to your ankle?"

"Oh, hi, Dr. William. It's a long story. I hurt it at Jake's house last night, just being my clumsy self."

"I'm sorry about that. Is there anything we can do for you?"

"How about letting me out of here early?"

"Well, that's what I wanted to talk to you about. A Minnetonka animal control officer just called. She's captured four raccoons, and she's bringing them over to us now. One of them bit a five-year-old girl, so she needs to know whether the animals are rabid. I'm sorry, but I'll need you to stay and help me, which should take about an hour. After we sedate them, we'll draw blood to verify the rabies and put them in separate cages. I'll pay you overtime and give you money for dinner, of course."

Beth Ann took a deep breath and forced a smile. "Sure, no problem, Dr. William. It'll be good experience for me."

"Thank you, Beth Ann. I knew I could count on you."

Beth Ann and Dr. William stood back from the cage. The momma raccoon was foaming at the mouth. She hissed and snarled, trying to protect her three cubs, who were huddled in the corner of the cage. "Poor things. They're so frightened," Beth Ann said.

"A classic case of rabies, unfortunately." Dr. Williams pointed to the mother. "Good thing it's so easy to order tranquilizer guns on Amazon these days. Saves a lot of people from getting bit by rabid animals." He filled the gun with morphine. With a gloved hand, he reached through the cage and injected the momma raccoon in her hindquarters. Within moments, she stopped hissing and fell limp. One by one, he repeated the process until all the babies were still.

Beth Ann helped him move each racoon into its own cage and draw a small vial of blood from each one. Dr. William locked the four cages and placed them in a larger cage with a sign that said "Stay Away. Rabid Animals." He pulled off his gloves and pointed at the now-empty tranquilizer gun. "Beth Ann, could you put that away? I'll be back in a moment."

She nodded and glanced at her watch. *Maybe I can still pick up Chipotle and make it to Jake's house for dinner.* Dr. William reappeared with an envelope in one hand and a $20 bill in the other. "This is a card for Jake. We heard about his stroke, and we've been keeping him in our prayers. Please give him a hug from all of us. And this is for you. Thank you for working late."

"Oh, Dr. William, you're welcome. I'm happy to help." She picked up her crutches and limped out to her car.

8

OMAR GLANCED OVER AT JAKE. "Hey, I wasn't kidding about chauffeuring you. You really shouldn't be driving, you know."

"What about the hospital's bullshit no driving policy that can't be enforced?" Jake snickered. "You said yourself it was nonsense."

"Yeah, well, I was desperate. And besides, you made it downtown in one piece."

"That's one in a row."

"Huh?"

"Listen, Omar, if you're going to drive for me, then don't bullshit me. That was the only one, and you don't get a second."

"Alleluia! I'm hired!" Omar took his hands off the wheel and shot them into the air. The Jag swerved into the other lane, nearly sideswiping the oncoming car.

"Goddamn it, Omar! Pay attention to your freakin' driving. Next time we're taking my SUV, not this guy—it's way too valuable."

"Geez Louise, Jake. I was just getting good at this stick shift." Omar pulled up alongside his Camry, at least what was left of it. The hood was open, the tires were gone, the windows were smashed, the inside was stripped, and the word niggur was spray-painted on the side. Omar double-parked, got out, and examined the car. "Son of a bitch, look at this. Gosh darn gangbangers couldn't even spell the word properly." Squatting down, he reached under the car. "Eureka!"

"What's going on?" Jake rolled down his window.

"Nothing, just those idiots missed a really nice SIG Sauer." He stuck the gun into the back of his pants and got back in the car.

"C'mon, Omar, what the hell do you need a handgun for? For God's sake, you're as big as a freakin' mountain."

"Yeah, but it gives me—and you—options."

Jake pointed to the Camry. "What about your car? Aren't you going to call a tow truck?"

"Nah, I only came back for the gun. I'm thinking it's a fair trade for this piece of shit." Already, some neighbors had come out of their houses and were pointing at them. A couple of tough-looking guys were striding towards them. Omar turned the key and pulled into the street. When the guys started running after them, he gunned the Jag and waved his middle finger over his shoulder. "As for my godforsaken rust bucket of a Toyota, it can sit there until the end of time. Hell, maybe those guys can even plant flowers in it!"

Jake navigated as Omar drove out to Victoria. Jake nodded at a Taco Bell on Highway 7, and Omar pulled into the drive-through. Jake ordered three Doritos® Locos Tacos

Supremes® with extra sour cream. Omar ordered six of the same, plus two Beefy Fritos® burritos and a large Mountain Dew. Since they were only ten minutes from Jake's house, they decided to wait and eat outside on Jake's deck. When they arrived, Omar looked around at the other houses and whistled appreciatively. "I could live here!"

Jake pressed the door opener and Omar pulled into the garage. He surveyed the collection of bicycles hanging on the wall. "So I guess you like to bike, eh, Jake?"

"Yeah, it's my favorite way to work out. My house backs up to a bike trail, which was one of the reasons I bought this place." He walked through the kitchen and out to the upper deck, with Omar trailing behind him. They sat down in comfy chairs that Beth Ann had given Jake for a housewarming present. Jake turned on the Sunbrite TV and opened the Taco Bell bag. Omar helped himself to a burrito and pointed to a biker on the trail.

"Aw, nice! I should get a bike. It'd probably help strengthen my bum leg."

"Yeah, it'd definitely help. You can borrow one of mine, but you'll have to be careful. There was a guy killed right down there last week." Jake pointed to the scarred oak and the remains of the yellow police tape and told Omar the story.

"Son of a gun, that's crazy. Do you honestly think saying 'Just die' made the guy crash?"

"Well, maybe I am crazy, but I'll tell you everything, and then you can decide." Jake finished the last bite of taco, stuffed the wrapper in the bag, and sat back in his chair. He explained how his mom had told him to point his finger instead of giving the finger, how his roommate at the hospital had died, how Kim Jong-un had keeled over on the tarmac, and how the biker had collided with the tree.

Omar listened intently until Jake was finished. "Is this some kind of joke? Are you saying you have some kind of mystical power that can make someone die, simply by pointing your finger at them and saying, 'Just die?'"

Jake sighed. "I don't know. Maybe it has something to do with my stroke."

"Yeah, well, maybe you need to chauffeur yourself. This is nuts." Omar pointed at a woman walking on the bike path. "If you really believe it, why not try it on her?"

Jake pointed his finger toward the woman. "Just... "

Jake looked at Omar and shook his head. "No way, Omar. I can't say it. What if it happens again?" They watched as the woman kept walking down the trail.

"God bless you, boss! Here's the thing. You're not killing people by saying 'Just die.' If I know one thing for sure, it's that strokes do weird things to people. Hell's bells, I've seen a guy who had a stroke, and depending on the day of the week, he thought he was either Jesus Christ or a bluebird. And hey, I didn't mean it when I said I wouldn't chauffeur you."

"Well, that's the best news I've heard all day. I do need you to keep driving me around, and I'm enjoying our conversations." The doorbell rang. "I'll get it. Probably an Amazon delivery or a couple of Jehovah's Witnesses. As long as I'm up, can I get you anything else?" Omar patted his stomach and shook his head.

Through the side window, Jake could see a man in a suit reaching out to ring the doorbell a second time. He opened the door to find two men who were clearly not Jehovah's Witnesses. The first guy was wearing a summer suit that must have cost a pretty penny. The second was wearing a shabby sport coat that looked like it came from a discount warehouse. The guy with the spiffy suit held up a gold detective badge. "We're here to see Mr. Jake Silver."

"That'd be me."

"I'm Detective Gino Sweeney, and this is my partner, Detective George Washburn. We're here because we'd like to have a word with you. Is now a good time?"

"Sure, come on in." The men stepped into the foyer, where they could see the well-appointed dining room, comfortable living room, and welcoming kitchen. "You have a beautiful home, Mr. Silver," Gino said.

"It must cost a fortune to keep your air conditioner this low," George said. "What exactly do you do for a living?"

Jake was just about to answer when Omar walked toward them. "Omar, these guys are detectives." Omar gave them a brief smile, and George looked at him with a glint of recognition.

"Gentlemen, let's be honest. Did you really come here today to admire my home and tell me to adjust my air conditioner?" Jake asked.

"No, sir, we're here to talk about the murder on the bike path," Gino replied.

"Wait. Did you just say murder?"

The detectives nodded, and Omar stepped closer to Jake.

"All right, then, but I'm not sure how much there is to tell. I was sitting on the deck with Beth Ann, my fiancée, when the accident happened, but she's at work right now."

The detectives nodded as if they already knew that. "Your fiancée? Well, congratulations. What's her name, if you don't mind me asking?" George pulled out a notebook and a pen and started writing.

"It's Beth Ann Noble."

"Could we see the deck?" Gino asked.

Jake looked at Omar, who gave a thumbs-up. The party filed out onto the deck, while Omar leaned against the door frame with his arms folded over his chest. Gino looked around and pointed at the oak tree with its banner of yellow police tape. George nodded, pulled a small camera out of his pocket, and snapped a few photos.

"So, Mr. Silver, I understand you had words with the biker," Gino said. He sat down in one of the deck chairs and Jake sat down across from him.

"Well, it was actually Beth Ann who spoke to him," Jake began. The memory was making him nauseous. "He was biking, and then he stopped to take a call. He was screaming and dropping a lot of f-bombs, so she leaned over the railing and yelled at him."

"What exactly did she say?" Gino asked.

"She told him to knock it off because we have young kids in the neighborhood. He gave her the finger and got back on his bike and rode off. But he was still yelling into his phone, so I'm thinking he must have been distracted, which may be why he crashed into the tree."

"That's it?" The detective looked sideways at Jake.

"I think so."

"She didn't yell 'Just die'?"

"Oh, no, that was me. That's what we do in our family. Instead of giving someone the finger, which creates road rage, my mom taught my siblings and me to point at them and say, 'Just die.'"

"Your mom sounds like a smart woman." Gino smiled. "According to your neighbors, you and your fiancée didn't check on the biker after he crashed."

"Well, we intended to, but then Beth Ann slipped on the wet leaves and twisted her ankle, so I helped her get back up to the house. We did call 911, though."

"Could I see your cell?"

Jake nodded and handed it to him. "But it was Beth Ann who called 911, so it would be on her phone."

"I'd still like to take a look at yours. Can I keep it for a few days?" Gino asked.

Jake snatched the phone back and slipped it into his pocket. "Heck, no, that's my only phone. I haven't had a landline in years."

George shot Jake a threatening look, but Gino simply shrugged. "I get that. I'd be lost without my cell too. Speaking of which, you said the biker was still on his phone when he veered off the path and crashed into the tree."

"Yes, that's correct."

"By chance, you and your fiancé haven't found the guy's cell, have you?"

"Heck, no. Don't you have it?"

"No, I'm afraid we haven't been able to find it, even though we've searched the area thoroughly."

"And did you happen to know the biker, Mr. Silver?"

Jake shook his head. "No, I've never seen him before in my life. He just happened to stop outside my house."

"So you weren't talking to him on your phone?"

Jake shook his head again, this time more vehemently. "No, of course not! And when Beth Ann spoke to him, she was leaning over the rail."

"Perhaps," George said under his breath.

Jake jumped up from his chair. "Look, as you probably know, I had just gotten home from 48 hours in the hospital after having a stroke. What's going on here, detectives?"

The detectives looked at each other. George shook his head, but Gino sighed and said, "Mr. Silver, I'll be honest with you, since I believe you've been honest with me. The guy on the bike is, I mean was, Dario Q. Mohammed. He had a criminal record with a long list of convictions for burglary and drug deals. The fact that he was outside your house wasn't random. His truck was parked in another neighborhood nearby, which is where he stole the bike he was riding. Based on everything we know, we believe you were his next target. You should count your blessings that he didn't break into your house and steal this nifty TV, your vintage Jaguar, and other valuables."

Jake's mouth dropped open, and he leaned forward in his chair.

"Dario Mohammed was a very dangerous man with equally dangerous friends," Gino said. "Now you know why we need to find his phone." He nodded to George, and the detectives stood up and moved toward the door, where Omar was still standing.

"I understand and I appreciate your honesty," Jake said. "I'll let you know if I come across anything that might help you." He walked the detectives to the front door and locked the door behind them. Jake returned to the deck, and he and Omar settled themselves around the table. "This is so strange," he said.

"Well, maybe not. Think about it. While you were in the hospital, your home was unattended, with no activity and no lights. This guy Dario probably knew someone who knew you had a stroke, so he was figuring you'd be gone for at least a week. Little did he know that clot-buster drug would have you back home in 48 hours."

"Wait, you think someone knew about my stroke and told Dario to rob me?"

"Why not? Could be someone with a taste for opioids or someone that doesn't like you."

"But everyone loves me, Omar. I mean, what's not to love?"

They laughed and high-fived each other. Moments later, Beth Ann appeared on the deck, holding a large Chipotle bag.

"Hi, guys! I hope you're hungry!" She leaned down and gave Jake a kiss. "Hi, Omar, nice to see you again! Thanks for taking such good care of Jake in the hospital."

Omar bowed slightly and took her hand and kissed it. "My pleasure. Your Jake is a good man, but you already know that."

"Believe me, I do. Now, who'd like a taco?"

9

PATIENCE WASN'T ONE OF DC'S virtues, and she was getting antsy. She'd parked her brand-new canary yellow Mazda convertible across the street from the veterinary clinic. To pass the time, she sipped on a flask of vodka, wincing. *God, I hate vodka. But it gets me through the day without anyone noticing.*

She looked out at the parking lot where her father's new Mercedes-Benz E 450 was, in its reserved spot, not far from Beth Ann's SUV. The Minnetonka animal control officer had left the clinic quite a while ago, so whatever her father and Beth Ann, or Big Ass, as DC called her, were doing was anybody's guess. *Maybe they're getting it on in the back room Big Ass is certainly very attractive, but she's too professional and not stupid enough for my dad. He prefers strippers with no brains and lots of makeup.* She took another sip of vodka and nearly gagged. *Shit, I could really use a fix right now.*

The clinic door opened. She watched as Beth Ann limped out to her SUV and drove off in a rush. Then Dr. William emerged and locked the door behind him. He began to punch in the key code but stopped. He shrugged and walked over to his car, looking around to make sure no one was watching. He fumbled with his zipper and then peed on his right front tire.

"Oh, gross!" DC groaned, putting her hands over her face. "I really didn't need to see that."

Dr. William took his time and then shook himself, smiling with relief as he opened the car door. He backed out of his spot and drove away.

▲ ▼ ▲

Jake remembered the Taco Bell bag on the kitchen counter. He snatched the bag, stuffed it into the garbage bin, and covered it so Beth Ann wouldn't see it. He returned to the deck with a six-pack of Diet Coke, a stack of paper plates, and a roll of paper towels.

Beth Ann was sitting next to Omar. She'd slipped his Super Bowl ring onto her ring finger and was holding it up to the sun. "My God, this is heavy! Just look at all those sparkles."

"It's the first Super Bowl ring to be made of platinum, not gold," Omar said proudly. "There are a total of 100 diamonds. The thirteen larger diamonds in the middle are for the thirteen championships the Packers have won."

"Wow. What's it worth?" Jake asked.

"Well, it depends. I'd never sell it, but it was appraised recently for $175,000. I know Lawrence Taylor's son sold off his dad's ring for more than $250,000. I have no idea if Lawrence even knew he was selling it."

Beth Ann passed the ring back to Omar and turned to Jake. "Hey, Omar told me about how you got him fired at the hospital and how he volunteered to be your driver. Shame on you!"

Jake looked sideways at Omar. "He told you I got him fired? Well, I'll be damned. So if you volunteered, that means I don't have to pay you, right?"

Omar grinned. "Whatever you say, boss! I'm just here to make my favorite Packers fan happy. As long as you guys keep feeding me tacos, we're good."

10

"SO, BETH ANN, WHAT DO YOU think about this whole 'Just die' thing?" Omar asked.

Beth Ann looked at Jake. "How much have you told him?"

"Practically everything. After all, since he's my personal chauffeur, he should know. But don't worry, he says it's just a coincidence and I'm nuts for thinking I have any special powers."

"Well, maybe Omar is right, but what if he isn't? He wasn't there when you told your roommate at the hospital to just die, and he wasn't there when you pointed at the TV and told Kim Jung-un to just die. She glanced over the railing and shuddered. "And he certainly wasn't here when that goddamn biker rode headlong into the oak tree."

"Now I'm thinking you're both nuts!" Omar said.

"Listen, Omar. Who are you to judge? Stranger things have happened!" Beth Ann said.

"Really? Name one!"

Beth Ann thought for a moment and snapped her fingers. "Well, how about the fact that the goddamn Packers have won thirteen championship titles and four Super Bowls, and the freakin' Vikings have won zero."

"Ha! She got you, Omar," Jake said, laughing.

Beth Ann gathered the remains of the dinner and stuffed it into the bag. "Tell you what, I know how we can put this 'Just die' crap to bed. We have four potentially rabid racoons at the clinic that are probably going to be euthanized tomorrow. If you're willing to come to the clinic with me tonight, we can test Jake's supernatural powers on the animals."

Jake shook his head. "No, I think Omar's right. This is all in my head."

"I don't know, Jake. I'm kind of intrigued by Beth Ann's idea. I think we should do it. We have to figure out if this thing is real, and we can't be testing it on humans."

Jake looked at a jogger running past the house on the bike trail and sighed. "You're right. Okay, Beth Ann, lead us to Rocky Raccoon."

▲ ▼ ▲

DC left her car on the street and hurried through the empty parking lot to the back door of the clinic. She keyed in the code, disabled the alarm, and locked the door behind her. Using the flashlight on her iPhone, she made her way through the clinic to the storage room where the prescription meds and narcotics were kept. She passed the room where the raccoons were being held, and the momma raccoon hissed at her through the open door. Startled, DC stuck her head into the room. Seeing the rabies sign on the cage, she closed the door.

When she reached the storage room, she took a ring of keys out of her pocket. A year ago, when she realized Dr. William kept a supply of morphine on hand, she'd stolen the keys from him. She used it only sparingly, since she preferred heroin, which she got from her friend Dario Q. Mohammed, a.k.a. Dairy Queen.

Hands trembling, she unlocked the door, flipped on the light, and locked the door again. She opened the cabinet door and smiled. Someone had thoughtfully restocked it with more than two dozen full syringes, so she grabbed a handful and set them on the desk. Wasting no time, she sat down in a chair and removed her right shoe. She used her sock to wipe between her big and second toes and stuck the needle in. She turned off the light, sat back, and waited for the rush. As the world disappeared into itself, her problems vanished, and she found herself hovering in a purple haze. She sighed with satisfaction. *This is the moment I live for!*

In her addled state, DC gazed up at Dr. William's diplomas, which proclaimed him a DVM, and giggled. "Little does he know he's really a doctor of veterinary morphine." She dearly loved her dad because he treated her like a queen. He bought her an apartment, leased a new car for her every two years, and gave her a generous salary and a monthly allowance. He'd never raised his voice to her and never disciplined her. But deep down inside, she knew it hadn't been good for her.

Apart from the obvious boundaries imposed by the teachers in her expensive private schools, DC had grown up without any guidance. But underneath her bleached blonde

hair and tattoos, she'd been one of the smartest kids in her
school. She was exceptionally good at math because it made
sense to her. If you broke the rules, you didn't get the right
answer. Simple as that. She also liked art, since she was
pretty good at drawing.

DC also excelled in gym class and played on the girls'
basketball team as a power forward. Even though she was an
average shot, she was a tenacious defender. But recalcitrant
by nature, she fouled at will. She always started the games,
but by halftime she was on the bench, fouled out of the
game. Her coach tried to curtail her attitude but eventually
gave up, so DC quit the team and filled her time with booze,
drugs, and occasionally, men, with little success, since none
of them treated her as well as daddy.

11

BETH ANN PULLED INTO THE clinic parking lot, which was, thankfully, empty. The trio got out of the Pathfinder and walked up to the back door. When she punched in the key code, she was surprised to find the alarm was off. "Hey, Jake, it looks like Dr. William forgot to set the alarm, so remind me to do it when I leave." She flipped on the lights in the reception area and led her companions to the examination room with the raccoon cages.

"I don't think I've ever seen a raccoon outside of a zoo. It's kind of cute," Omar said, peering into the cage. The raccoon snarled and lunged toward him. He jumped back. "Or not."

"Okay, you guys. Let's get this over with," Jake said. "Which one goes first?"

"The momma, but let's get the babies out of here," Beth Ann replied. She put on a pair of leather gloves and motioned to Jake and Omar to do the same. She opened the large cage, and they removed the smaller cages and carried them out to the hallway. Beth Ann pointed at a door. "We can stash them in this storage room for now." She tried the doorknob. "Duh, it's locked, which makes sense, since it's where we keep the meds. Okay, let's just leave them out here for now."

They went back into the room where the momma raccoon was beside herself, foaming at the mouth and throwing herself at the sides of her cage. "God, she reminds me of my ex-wife," Omar said as he backed into a corner. "Jake, do your 'Just die' magic and make it snappy, otherwise this poor creature is going to have a heart attack!"

Beth Ann touched Jake's elbow. "I'm kind of sorry I asked you to do this. You know, if it turns out you actually do have this power, your life could change in a heartbeat."

"Well, we all know I don't have any supernatural powers, so let's see what happens and then get the hell out of here." Jake pointed his finger at the raccoon. "Just die." He closed his eyes.

The momma raccoon had collapsed in a heap. Jake sat down in the chair and shook his head. "Now I don't know what to think."

"Yeah, this is freakin' weird. I wish I could say it was another coincidence," Omar said.

Beth Ann stared at the dead animal. "I really think you have the power, Jake. I mean, the human brain is remarkable, and who knows what that goddamn stroke did to you?"

"But how could a stroke give me the power to point my finger at something and make it die? Man, it just doesn't make sense!"

Omar shrugged. "Well, you've done it four times in a row, probably killing three people, including that biker, and definitely killing one raccoon."

"Well, I don't think it's a coincidence," Beth Ann said. But, to be sure, maybe you should do one of the babies."

"Aw, no way! They're too darn cute," Omar said.

"I agree with Omar. And besides, you don't know for sure whether the little ones are rabid." Jake replied.

"Good point. Let me see if the test results have come back," Beth Ann said, and left the room.

"You know, my sister Mary Jane lives up in northern Wisconsin," Omar said. "She and her husband have a small hobby farm with all sorts of critters. I know they have a god-awful time with the wild coyotes, so she'd probably love it if you'd point your magic finger at them."

Beth Ann walked into the room with a relieved smile. "Jake, you were right. The lab tests are normal for the little ones, so let's leave them alone. But momma was definitely rabid, so I'm kind of glad we put her out of her misery."

"So, what do we do now?" Omar asked.

"Nothing. Dr. William will send her to the crematorium tomorrow, and the babies will go to the wildlife rehabilitation center in Roseville."

"Okay, then. Let's get going," Jake said. "Omar has a good idea, so I'll let him explain it in the car."

"I'm all ears!" Beth Ann said with a smile.

▲ ▼ ▲

DC was drifting in and out of consciousness, floating on a fluffy silver cloud surrounded by sweet-smelling rose petals when her cell phone buzzed. She clumsily pulled the phone out of her pocket and looked at the name on the screen.

Dairy Queen.

Adrenaline surged through her body. She hit the accept button and started screaming. "Goddamn you, Dario! Where the fuck have you been? I'm going through withdrawal, and it's not a pretty sight. Son of a bitch! I need a goddamn fix!"

"Um, this is not, um . . . Mario," a youthful female voice said timidly.

"Then who the hell is it?" DC yelled.

"Well, if you're going to swear, I'm not telling you," the girl replied firmly.

DC took a deep breath and willed herself to calm down. "I'm very sorry. Please tell me who you are."

"I'm calling because I found this phone in a tree on the bike trail. Our dog Piglet was pooping, and I looked up and saw it stuck between a couple of branches. Luckily, I'm really good at climbing trees, so I went up there and brought it home and showed it to my mom. She told me to call you because this was the last number the person called. If you know how to reach them, I can return the phone and hopefully get a reward."

"Listen, miss, I'm sorry for swearing," DC said. "You did the right thing to call me. The phone belongs to my friend Dario, not Mario. He'll be really excited to get his phone back, and I'm sure he'll give you a reward. If you tell me your name and address, I'll come and get the phone."

"No, that's not what my mom wants me to do. She says if you're not Mario, we have to give it to the deputy in our town. He's really nice and he likes my mom's peanut butter cookies. Have a good day! Oh, and you really shouldn't swear so much. It makes people not like you," she said, and hung up.

DC's buzz was nearly gone now. *Goddamn it, where the hell is Dairy Queen? If he doesn't have his cell phone on him, that's a big problem. And if this little twerp gives it to that cookie monster of a deputy, that's an even bigger problem.* She spotted a McDonald's bag on the desk, which reminded her she hadn't eaten since the day before. She opened the bag and found an empty Big Mac container, an empty french fry bag, and a couple of cold fries. She ate the fries and dumped the rest in the garbage. She put the syringes in the bag and pulled her sock and shoe back on.

She was just about to leave when she spotted her cell phone on the table. *Crap, that would have been the kiss of death, leaving my fucking phone here.* She thought about calling the kid back, but decided against it in case the do-gooding mom answered. She opened the door into the hall.

She took one look at the baby raccoons in their cages and slammed the door shut. *What the fuck? I'm totally hallucinating. Must be the fucking morphine.* She took a deep breath and cracked the door open. *Damn, they're still there!*

Suddenly, another door to the storage room opened. Startled, DC pulled her door almost shut and peered through the crack. Big Ass emerged, followed by her sexy boyfriend Jake and the biggest black man she'd ever seen. She watched as they picked up the cages, then she closed her door and locked it. She couldn't hear what they were saying, so she grabbed a stethoscope and held it to the door She caught snatches of conversation from inside.

... I really think you have the power, Jake.

... point my finger at something and make it die?

... you've done it four times in a row, ... three people, including that biker, and definitely killing one ...

DC strained to hear more, but the trio was on their way out. She slumped against the wall. *What the hell was that? Am I still hallucinating? Did Big Ass's boyfriend really kill three people? How is that even possible?* She looked at the celling and closed her eyes. *Wait, what if he killed Dario?*

She stayed in the room for a few more minutes, then opened the door and peeked into the hall. Satisfied the coast was clear, she crept down the hall and opened the door to the storage room. She flipped on the light and frowned. Momma raccoon was as dead as a doornail, and the little ones were unconscious but breathing. Quickly making her way to the back door, she reset the alarm and left the clinic. She got in her car, stashed the McDonald's bag underneath her seat, and drove away.

As she headed down the frontage road, she spotted a liquor store conveniently located next to the McDonald's, where she bought a pint bottle of vodka and a small bottle of orange cognac. She got back in the car and took a hefty swig of the vodka and chased it with the cognac. She went through the McDonald's drive-through and ordered a double cheeseburger and two super-size fries with extra salt and lots of ketchup. She mashed the gas pedal and sped back to her apartment to sort out the last 24 hours and maybe take another hit of morphine. She had a bad feeling that Dario was no longer walking the Earth. That was a problem, since he was her only supplier.

▲ ▼ ▲

As they drove back to Jake's house, Omar explained his idea about the coyotes.

"I like it!" Beth Ann said. "The timing is perfect. I'll be done with school on Friday, and I'm sure Dr. William would give me a couple days off so we could head up to Wisconsin on Saturday morning."

"Cool," Omar said. "I'll text my sister and let her know. And since I'm the official chauffeur, I'll drive."

"You know, if your sister's place is in Bayfield County, it's probably not very far from our friends, the Fleischauers," Jake said. "I'll text them now and see if it's okay to stay in their cabin."

Right after breakfast on Saturday, they piled into Jake's SUV. Jake rode shotgun so he could navigate, and Beth Ann happily stretched out in the back seat. Omar opened up a plastic box and pulled out three stalks of celery spread thickly with peanut butter. He handed one to Jake and passed another to Beth Ann.

"What's up with the celery and peanut butter?" Beth Ann took a bite. "Didn't you guys get enough of it at the hospital?"

"Well, I must admit, it kind of grows on you, like fine scotch whiskey." Jake grinned. "Speaking of which, I hope Alan still has that bottle of 18-year-old Glenlivet in his booze cabinet."

"Hey, Silverado, if you're not supposed to be driving, you definitely shouldn't be drinking scotch," Omar said.

"Omar's right, Jake. And besides, I don't know why you don't just buy your own scotch."

"That's because drinking Alan's is way more fun. Omar, do you share my taste for single-malt whiskey?"

"Sure do, but it doesn't like me."

"What do you mean?" Beth Ann asked, leaning over the seat.

"Well, I pretty much quit cold turkey six years ago, and I've been sober ever since."

"More power to you, Omar," she said, gently punching him in the shoulder.

Jake helped himself to another stick of celery. "So, if you don't mind me asking, how'd you quit?"

Omar frowned. "Well, seeing as how you're my friends, and Jake is my boss, I'll answer the question. I did AA for a few weeks and then got fed up and quit. A bunch of people in those meetings were jerks, and all that higher power crap got to me. So I bagged going to the meetings and starting drinking Diet Coke, which now they're saying will kill you."

"Omar, that's bullshit." Beth Ann shook her head. "Jake and I drink it all the time. It's not going to kill us, or you."

Omar looked in the rearview mirror at the truck tailgating them. He moved over to the slow lane. The truck sped past and the driver gave him the finger. Jake pointed his finger at the rear of the truck, and Omar slapped his hand down. "Don't say it, boss, the guy's probably just in a hurry."

12

GINO WAS THE FIRST TO ARRIVE at the police station, as usual. It was casual Friday, so instead of an expensive suit, he was wearing khakis, a light blue short-sleeve shirt, and a pale blue linen sport coat. He made a pot of coffee, poured himself a cup, and grimaced. As part of his never-ending diet, he'd given up creamer and donuts. His coffee was now as black as the devil's nutbag and twice as bitter, so he added two packets of stevia, which was sweet, but nowhere near as satisfying as a glazed donut. As he sipped the coffee, he opened the local newspaper to the obituaries, as usual. *My God, young people are dying right and left.*

When his phone rang at 8 a.m., he set his coffee cup on the stained Vikings coaster and replied, "Sweeney."

"Officer Sweeney?" The person on other end of the line sounded like he needed his mother to drive him to work.

"Yes, this is Detective Sweeney."

"Um, this is Deputy Ralph McCray of the Victoria Sheriff's Department."

Gino smiled. He could sense that the deputy had something good to tell him. *This is going to be a good day. I can feel it in my bones.* "Yes, Deputy, how's your morning going so far?"

"Um, pretty good. Thanks for asking. So, my captain told me I should reach out to you, first thing this morning."

Gino waited.

"Well, so I patrol Victoria. And, um, my normal route has me going down Interlaken twice a day. That's the street that runs along the bike path."

Gino took another sip of coffee.

"Um, hello? Detective, are you still there?"

Gino closed his eyes, wishing he were eating a glazed donut. "Yep, I'm here, Deputy. How about you just spit it out?"

The deputy started talking so fast it seemed he was afraid he'd never get a chance to repeat the story. "Well, the other day, a resident flagged me down on Interlaken Street. Her name is Juliet Hanes, and she'd found her daughter Audrey talking to a boy from school on a cell phone. Problem was, Audrey doesn't have a cell phone, so Juliet immediately confiscated it and made her tell her how she got it. Turns out, Audrey was out walking their dog, Piglet, on the bike trail behind their house. When the dog stopped to take a poop, Audrey spotted the phone stuck in a tree branch, so she climbed up and retrieved it. When Juliet called the police to report it, my captain knew you were searching high and low for a cell phone that belonged to the guy who crashed into a tree on the trail, so he told me to call you."

Gino sat bolt upright in his deck chair, all thoughts of donuts vanishing from his mind. "Deputy, where are you right now?"

"Um, at the police station in Victoria."

"Good, can you meet me at the Hanes's house in, say, 45 minutes?"

"Sure, not a problem. Juliet's available until 11 a.m."

"Excellent. See you shortly. And make sure you have the phone with you."

▲ ▼ ▲

When Gino arrived at the Hanes's house, the officer opened the front door. He was holding the cell phone in his left hand and a peanut butter cookie in the right. "Good morning, Detective Sweeney, I'm Deputy McCray." He put the cookie in his mouth and reached out to shake the detective's hand.

Gino looked at the cookie crumbs clinging to the deputy's fingers and fist-bumped him instead. "Nice to meet you, Deputy. I assume this is the cell phone in question."

The officer grinned and handed the phone to the detective. "Yes, sir, it certainly is."

Gino took the phone and looked over the officer's shoulder. Juliet Hanes and a young girl and a younger boy were standing in the hallway that led to the kitchen. Gino stepped nimbly around the officer and greeted them. "Hi there, I'm Detective Gino Sweeney from the Minnetonka Police Department."

"Well, welcome! I'm Juliet, and this is Audrey and Griffin. I don't think we've ever met a real live detective, right, kids?"

"Well, now you have. Great job finding the phone, Audrey."

"Do detectives carry guns?" Griffin asked.

"Yes, we do, but we only use them when we don't get peanut butter cookies."

"Oh, no." Audrey knitted her brow. "I'm afraid the officer ate the last one."

Gino winked at the kids. "Well, then, I guess I'm going to have to shoot him. What do you think about that?"

Audrey giggled. "Oh, no, don't do that. He's nice."

"Well, even though we don't have any more cookies, we do have some warm brownies and fresh coffee in the kitchen," Juliet said.

"That'd be just fine." Gino followed her and the kids into the kitchen, and the deputy brought up the rear. The men sat down, and Juliet set a platter of brownies next to a small pitcher of cream and a bowl of real sugar. She filled two mugs with coffee and put them on the table. Gino helped himself to the cream and sugar.

Like Jake's house, the Hanes's kitchen opened onto a deck that overlooked the bike trail. Gino looked at Audrey. "So, I heard about how you found the cell phone, and I'm happy to say that you'll be getting a reward for your bravery. But I'm also interested in hearing from your mom about the mur... I mean, when the man crashed into the oak tree."

"Well, I'm sure you've already heard the story from Jake and Beth Ann," Juliet said. "But we were sitting here at this table when I heard someone yelling on the bike path, so I went out on the deck. There was a man in a hoodie on a bike right below Jake's house. He was screaming into a cell phone, swearing to beat the band and hollering the f-word. I was just about to speak up, but Beth Ann jumped right in before I could say anything. She let the guy have it, telling him to knock it off since there were young kids in the neighborhood. And God bless her for that."

"So then what happened?" Gino asked.

"The guy looked up and gave her the finger. She was just about to give it right back to him, but then she stopped. Jake said something, but I couldn't hear it. When the guy got back on his bike and rode away, Jake leaned over the railing, pointed his finger, and yelled at him."

"Did you hear what he said?" the detective asked.

Juliet hesitated. "Yes, he said, 'Just die.'"

▲ ▼ ▲

Omar pulled into the Fleischauers' driveway and parked the SUV in the gravel-covered car park. The friends picked up their duffels and went inside. Beth Ann went in search of Diet Coke while Jake gave Omar the tour. The cabin had a master bedroom, a guest room, and a kitchen, as well as a great room with overstuffed lounge chairs and a 60-inch TV. Omar plopped down in one of the chairs and surveyed the rustic décor. "Wow, this is really nice. Whoever decorated this has a wonderful eye."

"That'd be Alan's wife, Paula." Beth Ann grinned as she passed around the drinks.

"So, Omar, what's the plan with your sister?" Jake asked.

"I said we'd be there around ten tomorrow morning. According to Google, it's about an hour's drive from here."

"Perfect. That'll give Jake plenty of time to make his famous eggs Benedict for breakfast."

"Oh, no, I can't make breakfast. I just had a stroke."

"I call bullshit!" Omar said with a laugh. "Let's go outside and sit on the deck. I want to check out the views. What lake are we on?"

"It's called Cranberry Lake, only it's really a bay," Jake explained. "There are only six cabins and two permanent residents. Most of these folks are from Chicago, so they don't get up here as much as Alan and Paula. And since you have to go through another bay called Crystal Bay to get to Namekagon Lake, there's not a lot of boat traffic on Cranberry, which is really nice."

"It's fantastic. It feels like I'm in Canada with all these giant pine trees." At that moment, a red squirrel ran up the trunk of a 70-foot red pine next to the deck.

"Goddamn red squirrels." Beth Ann scowled.

"Aw, come on, I like squirrels," Omar said.

"We do too, but only the gray ones," Jake replied. "Red squirrels are nasty pests. They're highly invasive, they make nests in people's attics, and they're basically a pain in the proverbial rear end."

"He's right," Beth Ann said. "There's a saying up here in the north woods. 'Gray, you stay; red, you die,' which is usually followed by a 12-gauge shotgun blast that drops the red squirrel right out of the tree."

Omar cocked his head at the squirrel. It was sitting on a branch, looking down at them with what looked like a smirk on its tiny face. Beth Ann tapped Jake's arm and pointed to the squirrel. Jake hesitated, then raised his hand and pointed at the rodent. "Just die," he said under his breath.

The squirrel somersaulted off the branch and fell to the ground. Omar looked over the railing and pronounced the critter dead. "You know, boss, if this keeps happening, I'm going to side with Beth Ann. I'm thinking you really do have the power."

"I'm afraid you may be right." Jake hung his head. "And if you're right, it really sucks."

"Oh, no, I disagree," Beth Ann said. "Think of all the evil people in this world who deserve to be eliminated."

"And respectfully, I disagree with you, Beth Ann," Omar said. "I'm with Jake on this. Wicked people have sharp teeth, and if they find out about Jake's powers, he's a dead man walking."

"Holy shit, Omar, I'm afraid you're right." Jake stood up and disappeared into the cabin.

"No way." Beth Ann shook her head. "That's just goddamn bullshit. Just think about what Jake could do with this God-given power. After all, he may have already killed Kim Jong-un, probably one of the most evil men on Earth."

"Yeah, but what happens when Putin hears about it?"

Jake reemerged, pushing open the deck's screen door. He had a can of Diet Coke under his arm, a glass of wine in one hand, and a cocktail glass in the other. He handed the wine to Beth Ann and the Diet Coke to Omar. He sat down in his chair, raised his glass in the air, and took a sip. "Cheers. If I'm a dead man walking, I sure as hell deserve to drink the world's finest scotch whiskey!"

13

ON SUNDAY MORNING, THE TRIO arrived at Omar's sister's place. Omar parked near the house, and they got out so he could show them around. He'd described it as a hobby farm, but in reality, it was a working farm. There were three barns, two small and one large. Behind the large barn, there were a couple of chicken coops and an immense vegetable garden. Four dairy cows stood in a copse of trees, a stand of beef cattle grazed in one field, and a half-dozen horses cavorted in another.

A woman opened the door and waved. She was smiling broadly and holding a mug with a Packer logo, but she set it down on the railing so she could give Omar a hug.

"Mary Jane, these are my friends Beth Ann and Jake," Omar said. "You guys, meet my favorite sister, Mary Jane Michaud."

"Welcome! I just made a fresh pot of coffee, so come on into the kitchen and we can get acquainted." Beth Ann gave Jake a quizzical look as they followed Mary Jane into the farmhouse, because, unlike her brother, Mary Jane was white. She led them into a spacious kitchen that smelled of baking. She set an old-fashioned percolator on a trivet and arranged a plate of chocolate chunk cookies and three more Packer mugs on the table. "Oh, Omar, it's so good to see you. It's been way too long."

"Sure has, Sis. It's been nearly a year.".

"I suppose you two are wondering why I'm white and not black like Omar," Mary Jane said. "I knew he wouldn't mention it, since he doesn't like to share his stories. We're both adopted, and we have a sister who lives with our mother. Her name is Asha Jade Wong, and she's half Japanese and half Korean. Our parents couldn't conceive, so they went shopping, as my father used to say."

"That's funny," Beth Ann said. "Thanks for sharing. Omar, I hope you don't mind."

"Nah, I trust you guys," Omar said. "Now, where's Tom?"

"Oh, he's in his happy place, playing with his beloved horses. He just bought a new one to replace Pete. The damn coyotes got Pete, and he had to be put down since the coyotes were rabid." At the mention of rabies, Jake looked sideways at Beth Ann, and she nodded.

"Omar! A little bird told me you were here!" An older man wearing a tan Open Road Stetson with a sheriff's star on the black leather band marched into the kitchen, and Omar jumped up and hugged him. "Jake, Beth Ann, meet my other favorite brother-in-law, John Michaud."

Jake stood up and shook John's hand. "Nice to meet you, John. I'm Jake Silver, and this is my fiancée, Beth Ann." John tipped his hat toward Beth Ann.

"Nice to meet you both. Mind if I join you? I do love Mary Jane's cookies, and it's been a long time since

breakfast. Omar says you can help Tom and Mary Jane
tackle the coyotes, which would be much appreciated. I just
came from George Hijack's place, and those damn coyotes
snatched a steer and a one-year-old calf in broad daylight
yesterday."

"Oh, no, not Bully, I hope," Mary Jane said.

"Yep, I'm afraid so. George paid a hell of a price for
her."

"That's terrible."

"Indeed it is. So, Jake, how are you going to kill these
buggers?" John asked. "I took a look in that nice SUV of
yours, and I didn't see any guns or traps."

"That's because Jake's going to tell them to die," Omar
said. "He points at them and says, 'Just die!'—and they do!"

"Oh, now, that's funny, Omar," Mary Jane said. "But
seriously, what is Jake planning to use? Some kind of
poison?"

Just then, Tom Michaud appeared in the doorway.
"Omar, I heard what you said, and it's not funny. We're
having a serious problem with these creatures, and I'm at my
wits' end."

Jake stood up. "You'll just have to trust me." He walked
out of the kitchen. The rest of the gang followed him as he
hurried down the stairs to his SUV. He pulled out a duffel
bag, stripped off his shirt, put on a hunting shirt, and slid his
camo pants over his shorts. "Tom, can you put out some

bait and set me up so I have a clear sight line to the coyotes?"

"No need for bait. They're circling the cows right now."

"C'mon everyone. Let's get this show on the road." Jake strode through the tall grass toward the field, wondering again about the wisdom of what he was doing. *Maybe Omar is right. If so, it'll only be a matter of time before someone puts a mark on me.*

▲ ▼ ▲

DC was coming off a high. But instead of floating in a pretty purple hazy high, she'd been dreaming of rude little girls, cell phones, f-bombs, and police officers. Her eyes popped open, and she looked around the room. She had no idea how long she'd been out of it. Her mouth tasted like crap, and she was dying of thirst. She reached for the Mountain Dew can on the table, took a hefty swallow, and immediately began to choke. She jumped up, rushed to her bathroom, and vomited into the toilet.

She kneeled over the toilet, looking at the remains of a double cheeseburger and two super-sized fries with extra ketchup. She reached up, pulled the lever, and flushed the mess out of sight. She yanked a towel off the rod, wiped her mouth, curled up on the mat, and dozed off again.

She woke up a couple of hours later. She brushed her teeth to get rid of the nasty taste, gargled twice with mouthwash, and staggered into her bedroom. The sun was streaming through the window, which surprised her. Last she remembered, she was shooting up and it was dark outside. She glanced at the clock on the bedside table and was surprised to see that it was 11:30 a.m. At that moment, the phone rang, and she breathed a sigh of relief when she saw Dario's name.

Thank God!

"Dairy Queen, where the fuck have you been?"

"Ms. Krueger?" A male voice thundered through the phone, and she suddenly remembered everything that had happened the day before.

"Uh, yes, this is DC Krueger. Who is this?"

"This is Detective Gino Sweeney of the Minnetonka Police Department. I'm afraid I have bad news about your friend, Dario Q. Mohammed."

DC rocked back on her heels. "Oh, no, what happened?"

The detective paused for effect. "I'm sorry to say he's dead."

DC pulled the phone away from her ear and stared at it. *Dario is dead? Oh, shit.*

"Ms. Krueger, are you still there?" the man asked.

"Who did you say you are?" DC stalled, her mind racing.

"Detective Gino Sweeney from the Minnetonka Police Department. And while I'm sorry about your loss, I need to speak with you immediately about your friend."

DC gathered her wits. "Listen, Detective, I don't know anyone named Mario. You have the wrong person, so please don't call me anymore."

Gino laughed. "Well, Ms. Krueger, I'm afraid that's not exactly true. I'm holding a phone that belonged to Dario, not Mario, and based on his recent calls, you two appear to have known each other well."

There was a loud rap on DC's door. "I'm sorry, Detective, but there's someone at my door, so I have to go."

"Ms. Krueger, two of the finest police officers in Hopkins are at your door. They're going to invite you to meet me at the Minnetonka police headquarters this afternoon. As I'm sure you know, it's on Minnetonka Boulevard just off of Highway 494."

DC swore under her breath and peered through the peephole. Sure enough, two cops, a male and a female, were standing at her door, with the apartment manager right behind them. *No wonder they didn't use the buzzer to get in. They went straight to the old biddy, who I'm sure is loving all this drama.*

"DC, are you still there?" Gino asked.

"Yeah, I'm still here, and you're goddamn right. There are two officers right outside my door, and so what? This is my home, and I don't have to open the door to anyone—and that includes cops!"

Shit, DC, that was a dumb-ass thing to say. She peeked through the spy hole again. The apartment manager had her keys in her outstretched hand, and the officers were moving aside. Before the manager could unlock the door, DC grabbed the knob and opened it herself. She put the phone on speaker so the visitors could hear her. "Okay, Mr. Detective," she shouted into the phone. "You'll be happy to know I'm opening the door, and I'll meet you at your freakin' police headquarters. But not right now. I'll be there at 2 p.m."

"That'd be fine," Gino said. "And make sure you bring your cell phone with you."

The officers nodded and walked down the hall, the apartment manager pestering them with questions.

14

JAKE CLIMBED ONTO THE WHITE wooden fence and sat on the top rail. He had an unobstructed view of the cows, who appeared to be blissfully unaware of the danger lurking around them. To his untrained eye, they all looked alike. He knew next to nothing about dairy cows, but he'd heard Beth Ann talk about Guernseys, Holsteins, and other breeds.

He looked over his shoulder to watch Tom firing up the grill and caught the flash of a coyote. Goddamn, John wasn't exaggerating when he said the coyotes were hunting in broad daylight. He guessed the one he had seen was the leader, and, sure enough, nearly a dozen coyotes were following the animal into the field.

The leader looked to be in fairly good shape, but the others were scrawny and mangy. A couple were limping, having likely escaped a trap. A shiver ran through Jake when the lead coyote made a run for the cows. It was now or never. He remembered one of his father's favorite phrases, "Put up or shut up," and decided to put up. Straightening his shoulders, he set his sights on the lead coyote, pointed his finger, and shouted, "Just die!"

Just like momma raccoon, the coyote collapsed in a heap less than a yard from the cows. Three other coyotes stopped abruptly, which Jake used to his advantage. One by one, he pointed at them.

"Just die!"

"Just die!"

"Just die!"

The animals dropped like flies, and the rest of the pack sensed danger. They turned and ran toward the distant forest in a tight cluster. Wiggling all his fingers on both hands at the retreating coyotes, Jake shouted "Just die!" over and over, until every last one was dead.

Trembling, he gazed at the results of his efforts. Thankfully, the cows were still standing, waving their tails complacently. He sniffed the air and turned around. Flames were leaping up from the grill, but the bystanders were all oblivious. Everyone was leaning over the deck railing and counting the dead coyotes.

Jake swung his legs back over the fence and ran toward the deck. By that time, Tom had noticed the grill fire. He put the lid back on, and the fire was under control. Jake jogged over to the SUV, and Beth Ann helped him take off his camo. She folded his shirt and pants neatly, put them in his duffel, and stowed it in the back of the SUV. She turned to him with tears streaming down her face. "Oh, my God, Jake. What have we done?"

▲ ▼ ▲

DC was also crying, slumped on her sofa. *Why me? Why does this shit always happen to me? And what the hell am I going to do without Dario?* She thought back to her last conversation with him and got a weird sense of *déjà vu.*

She had been sitting in the same place, screaming at him on the phone. "Fuck you, Dario! Whaddya mean, Jake is sitting on his deck? He's supposed to be in the hospital. The dumbass just had a stroke two days ago!"

"Well, I'm standing here on the bike path, and I can see a guy and a girl on the deck, and she just called him Jake."

"That's impossible, Dario. Fuck you."

"Bullshit, and fuck you too!"

DC was just about to retort when she heard Dario yelling at someone else. "Dario, what's happening?"

"Listen, DC, I can't talk right now. I've gotta get out of here and get my damn truck. And in the meantime, go to hell. I don't need your bullshit anym..."

DC heard a loud crash. "Dario? Dario? Talk to me. Are you okay?"

Now realizing her worst nightmare was fast becoming reality, DC curled up in the corner of her sofa, shaking. *Shit, I've got no backup dealer, and I have to meet that fucking detective in two hours.* Taking a deep breath, she pulled herself together, picked up her phone and scrolled through her contacts. When she reached Scott Knewely, her father's divorce attorney, she pressed the call button.

Scott answered on the second ring. "Well, hello, DC! To what do I owe the pleasure of your call? You're not in the market for a divorce, are you? Last time I saw you, you didn't even have a boyfriend."

"Hey, Scott. No, I'm not, and thankfully, neither is my dad, at least at the moment. But I'm in a jam, and I could use some wise counsel, and you're the only lawyer I trust. Hell, you're the only lawyer I know."

"I'm sorry, DC, I was just messing with you. How can I help?"

Scott listened as DC explained how Dario had crashed while he was on the phone with her. She told him how the girl called from his phone and how the officers showed up at her apartment, wanting to know more, but she left out the part about the drugs and the attempted burglary. *No need to share everything.*

"Well, DC, I'm sure it's all a misunderstanding. You'll definitely want to cooperate with the police, but my partner, Tim Murray, is a defense attorney, and he's the best."

"Defense attorney? Why would I need him?"

"If you're meeting with the police today, you should have a defense attorney with you, and I'm only a divorce attorney. Let me call Tim now and see if he can meet you at the police station."

"Oh, Scott, I don't want Tim. I need you to be there."

"Listen, trust me on this. You definitely need Tim Murray, but if you insist, I'll be there as well to support you, okay?"

"Okay, Scott. Thank you." DC wiped away a tear and gazed around at her disheveled apartment. *This is a goddamn mess.* She put on her headphones, opened her trusty flask of vodka, took a swig, and swung into action. Flask in one hand and vacuum in the other, she rocked out to a Spice Girls song.

When she was finished, she looked at the McDonald's bag of morphine on the table but decided against it. She took a shower, picked out a pretty flowered summer dress from her walk-in closet, put on some makeup, and looked at herself in the mirror. *Hey, I clean up pretty damn well.* She took another swig.

She glanced at her cell phone and debated whether to take it with her. The fact that the detective had ordered her to bring it irked her. But she was also afraid not to bring it, so she put it in her purse. She grabbed the flask and a syringe of morphine, went out to her car, and stowed the items in the glove box. Roaring off to the Minnetonka police station, she didn't notice the two police officers parked in an adjacent lot.

The officers, who were the same ones who'd knocked on DC's door, pulled out of the lot and covertly followed her car. "Looks like she's headed over to you," one of the officers said to Gino, "and she's got a lead foot, so she should be there in a moment. See you in a few."

DC sped down Minnetonka Boulevard and turned down the long, curving driveway that led to the rear of the Tonka cop shop, as the locals called it. She parked in the far corner of the lot and looked around to make sure no one was watching. She opened the glove box and took one last drink of vodka before locking her car.

She made her way to the reception area, where a woman sat behind the counter, protected by a sheet of thick, bulletproof glass. "How can I help you?" the woman asked without smiling.

"I'm DC Krueger, and I'm here to see Detective Sweeney."

The receptionist nodded. "Yes, he's expecting you. If you wait in the lounge area, someone will be out to meet you shortly."

A good-looking man in a tan suit was sitting on one of the sofas. Smiling, he said, "Excuse me, are you DC Krueger?" He stood up and extended his hand. "I'm Tim Murray, and I'm here to represent you at the behest of Scott Knewely."

DC looked him up and down with a practiced eye. He looked just like a young Robert Redford. If you filled those goddamn dimples with water, you could swim laps. "Why, yes, I am," she said sweetly, suddenly very glad she had taken Scott's advice. "I'm certainly happy to meet you."

15

JAKE AND BETH ANN WALKED over to the stairs, where
Omar was standing on the top step. His face looked grim.
He reached out and shook Jake's hand. "I'd say nice job, but
holy smoly, Jake. After that performance, the shit is going to
hit the effing fan."

Jake looked across the deck to where John was standing
alone, his Stetson in his hand. He had a perplexed look that
reminded Jake of a cardsharp's poker face. If Jake had to
guess, John appeared to be deciding whether he should go
all in.

"Jake, I bet you've worked up an appetite. How about a
hot dog or two? I hope you like 'em black and crispy!"

Everyone laughed. "If it's okay with you, Tom, I'd like to
sit down and have a beer or two," Jake said. "But let's skip
the blackened wieners!"

"Sounds good." Tom laughed and shut the grill cover.
"After that performance, I could use a beer myself." Mary
Jane sat down next to Jake and patted his hand. "Jake, I
don't know what you've gotten ahold of, but my God, what a
wonderful gift! You can change the world with this. Think of
all the farmers and ranchers you can help by getting rid of
coyotes and other predators. This is life changing—not only
for you, but the entire world!"

"Mr. Silver, you need to explain to me what we just saw," John said. "This gift you seem to have is not of this world, unless I'm actually at home in my bed and dreaming. Please tell me I am."

▲ ▼ ▲

DC shook Tim's hand. He wasn't wearing a wedding ring, so she immediately began making plans for a big wedding.

The door opened to reveal George Washburn. "Tim, what the hell are you doing here?" he asked with a scowl.

"Long time no see, Burnsey!" Tim was grinning. "I haven't seen you since you damn near perjured yourself on the stand."

"That's bullshit. The woman was guilty and you know it," George snarled.

"Oh, really? Is that why the judge threw the case out into the freaking interstate and then petitioned your boss to have you terminated?"

George closed the door. "Oh, fuck you, Mr. Sleazebag Harvard Attorney. I'm still here, and you best watch your back. This is my territory."

Tim winked at DC. "My friend Burnsey's a really nice guy if once you get to know him."

George spun on his heel and led Tim and DC into a conference room. "Yazus H. Christmas on a freakin' pogo stick. What the hell are you doing here, Tim?" the man inside demanded.

"Take it easy, Gino. This is simply a meet-and-greet, and no one's being charged with anything. Ms. Krueger was willing to come down here of her own free will, and she damn well doesn't need an attorney."

DC took a seat at the table opposite Gino, George sat down at the head, and Tim sat down next to Gino. "It's good to see you, Detective. How's your family?" Tim asked with a grin.

"My family's just fine, Counselor, and even if they weren't, it's none of your goddamn business!" Gino snarled.

"Well, I think my associate Scott Knewely might take exception with that statement. He tells me that your lovely wife is divorcing you and suing the Minnetonka Police Department. Sounds to me like they plan on taking every nickel you've ever made—and ever will."

Gino grabbed Tim by the front of his shirt. "Goddamn you, you asshole, you leave my family out of this."

"For Chrissakes, Gino, be a professional. You're making a fool of yourself." Tim removed Gino's hand from his shirt. "Now chill out. I'm delivering Ms. Krueger to you at your request, so let's get this over with." He winked at DC. "And then maybe I'll take us all to Dairy Queen."

Gino reluctantly backed off of Tim.

"I need to remember to wear a bow tie around you, Detective," Tim said with a smirk. "Now, whether you like it or not, Ms. Krueger is being represented by my firm. I assume you have some questions, so have at it."

"So, Ms. Krueger, how do you know Dario Q. Mohammed?" Gino began.

DC opened her mouth to speak, but Tim nudged her. "Let me do all the talking for now," he whispered. He turned to Gino. "Why do you want to know?"

Gino rolled his eyes. "Okay, fine. So that's how this is going to go. And now that I think about it, I suppose that's a fair question. Mr. Dario Q. Mohammed, who is now deceased, was in Ms. Krueger's cell phone contacts. And from what we can tell, he was talking to her when he ran headlong into an oak tree on a bike trail in Victoria."

"That's tragic, but you're mistaken," DC broke in. "Dario wouldn't know a bicycle from a bulldozer."

"So you did know him!" Gino said with a grin. Tim nudged DC again. "Well, in addition to being a known burglar, a dope dealer, and a bad guy all around, he must have been a fast learner, because he died while riding a bike, which was stolen from a home along the bike path."

"Mr. Mohammed's truck was parked on the street near the home of Jake Silver," George chimed in. "And Mr. Silver's fiancée, Beth Ann Noble, is a colleague of Ms. Krueger. They work together at a veterinary clinic owned by Ms. Krueger's father."

Gino shook his head at George, who stopped talking and looked down at his notepad.

"So fucking what?" Tim shrugged.

"I'll tell you fucking what, Counselor," Gino said. "Do you know that Jake Silver had a stroke?"

DC whispered something into Tim's ear.

"Yes, Ms. Krueger does know that," Tim said. "She expressed her condolences to his fiancée while they were at work."

"Well, Counselor, I didn't go to Harvard Law School, but this is also not my first fucking rodeo," Gino said. "So here's how I see it. Mr. Silver was in the hospital, so Ms. Krueger reached out to her good friend Mr. Mohammed and suggested he go over to Mr. Silver's house and rip off a couple of expensive TVs. But unbeknownst to Mr. Mohammed, Mr. Silver had been discharged from the hospital earlier that afternoon. So, when Mr. Mohammed saw him and his fiancée on the deck, he called Ms. Krueger, and, while he was berating her, he crashed into the tree."

"That's a fucking lie!" DC shouted.

"Allow me to finish, Ms. Krueger," Gino said. "Based on several interviews with your coworkers and friends, it would appear that you're a drug user and Mr. Mohammed was your supplier."

"For Chrissakes, Detective, that's a stretch and you know it, so let's conclude this session." Tim stood up.

"Not so fast, Counselor," Gino said. "Ms. Krueger, do you have your cell phone with you? George and I would like to take a look at it."

DC glanced at Tim, and he shook his head.

"Okay, then, no cell phone," Gino said. "How about if you voluntarily submit to a drug test on the taxpayers' nickel? If you aren't using, we'll apologize to both of you and most likely leave you alone."

"Are you out of your mind, Detective?" Tim said. He glared at Gino and opened the door.

▲ ▼ ▲

Tom popped the top on a bottle of Spotted Cow beer and handed it to Jake, who took a long swig before replying to John.

"No, John, you're not dreaming, but to be honest, this is shaping up to be my worst nightmare. I'm going to tell you all a story that you may well not believe. Hell, I'm having trouble believing it myself. But unfortunately it's true, and I don't know what to do about it." Jake took another long swig and sighed heavily. "It all started when I was 16 years old and learning to drive. No matter what the other drivers did, my mother wouldn't let me give them the finger because she said it would only cause road rage. Instead, she taught me to point my finger at the offending driver and whisper, 'Just die,' under my breath. They didn't die, of course, but ever since I had a stroke, things have been different.

Tom handed him a second beer, and Jake launched into the rest of the story. He explained about the day his roommate in the hospital died, and how, shortly after, Kim Jong-un had collapsed on the tarmac. He told them about the encounter on the bike path, the rabid raccoon, and the red squirrel in the pine tree at the Fleischauers' cabin. "And now the coyotes."

John shook his head in amazement. "Well, if I hadn't seen it with my own eyes, I'd never have believed it. But goddamn it, I did see it, and there's no way to unsee it."

"Hey, Jake, if it makes you feel any better, Kim Jong-un didn't die," Tom said. "Apparently, he just fainted."

"Well, that's good news, I think," Jake replied.

"Nah, you should have killed him. I'm more worried about him than a bunch of coyotes."

"Well, Jake, as I said before, I think you have a God-given gift," Mary Jane said. "But it's ultimately up to you whether you want to share it with the world."

"I'll tell you what," John said. "If I had this kind of power, I'd probably hide it and never tell a soul. Hell, I might even go back to flipping people off again!"

"I appreciate all your good thoughts, but I really need to spend some time thinking about this," Jake said with a sigh. "Maybe this really is a gift and I should do something with it. But present company excepted, who's going to believe me? And who knows how long my abilities will last. A week? A month? Forever? It's a lot to process, so if you don't mind, I'm ready to call it a day."

After several rounds of hugs, Jake, Omar, and Beth Ann climbed into the SUV. When Omar reached the turnoff for the Fleischauers' cabin, Jake pointed at a sign for the Loon Saloon. "Hey, let's stop here. They have great pizza, some decent scotch, and a pool table."

"Sounds good to me!" Beth Ann said.

"No scotch for me, but I'll beat your proverbial butt at pool!" Omar said. The trio walked into the saloon. They sat by the window, where they could see Lake Namekagon sparkling in the late afternoon sunlight.

"Hi, folks, I'm Mary!" the bartender said. She looked at Omar and then at Jake. "If you're getting pizza, you best get a couple of extra slices for your friend here."

Omar laughed. "I'm getting a whole pizza for myself. I hear your house special is wonderful, so I'll take one of those, extra crispy, and a Diet Coke."

"Make that two house specials and two more Diet Cokes," Beth Ann said. "Mary, meet our good friend Omar. This is his first visit to the Loon."

"Nice to meet you, Mary." Omar stuck out his hand. "Nice place you have here."

"Welcome! Glad you like it. It's for sale, if you happen to be in the market for a saloon. No pool table, though."

"Where'd it go?" Jake asked.

"I gave it to a senior living facility in Hayward. It got to be more trouble than it was worth, what with the drunken fishermen gouging the felt and spilling beer all over it."

"That's actually good news for you guys," Beth Ann said. "If Mary still had her pool table, I'd have beaten both of your sorry asses!"

16

AFTER TIM AND DC LEFT, GINO looked at George
Washburn and frowned. On one hand, George was a good
note taker. On the other, he was the dumbest detective Gino
had ever encountered. Not for the first time, Gino wondered
how George had passed his detective exams. But then again,
George's father was commissioner of the Minneapolis police
force, so that may have had something to do with it.

"I didn't know you talked to Ms. Krueger's friends and
coworkers," George said.

"I didn't," Gino replied. "I just needed to shake her up a
bit, and that was the only theory that held up, in my mind.
I'll bet your pension she uses drugs on a regular basis. So
here's what I want you to do. Keep her in sight and get a
Hopkins black and white to follow her home. Just before
she gets there, have them pull her over, check her car, and
report back."

▲ ▼ ▲

In the parking lot, DC put her hand on Tim's arm. "Thanks
for your help, Tim."

"You're very welcome. But we need to talk. Gino's a
homicide detective, and he would not be screwing around

with a man on a bike path unless he smells murder. So, you have to be straight with me. If you're using, I need to know. Think about that, and I'll see you tomorrow at 10 a.m. sharp, in my office."

DC was only half listening to what Tim was saying because she was envisioning their honeymoon. *Hawaii? Maybe, but nowhere touristy like Maui. Or Costa Rica? Nosara might be nice. Or how about a week in Paris and another week exploring the nude beaches in the south of France? Yes, now we're talking!*

"Ms. Krueger, are you listening to me?" Tim waved his hand in front of her.

"Sure, meet you at your office at 10 and don't do drugs, right?" She slid behind the wheel of her car and rolled down her window. "Hey, Tim, have you ever been to Paris?"

Tim just smiled and walked back to his car. DC opened her glove box and eyed the syringe. Shooting up in the parking lot of police HQ is probably not a good idea. She took out her flask, thumbed off the cap, tipped it to her mouth, and gagged. *Goddamn, that shit is terrible.* She tossed the empty flask onto the passenger seat and headed out of the parking lot. *That fucking Dario. Selfish prick. How dare he up and die on me? Now I need a new dealer.*

Lost in thought, she didn't notice the squad car that was tailing her.

▲ ▼ ▲

What an idiot, George thought as he spotted a flash of sunlight reflecting off DC's aluminum flask. He pulled out of the lot, then took his foot off the gas and allowed several cars to get in between her canary yellow Mazda and his unmarked green Ford Impala. His car was ten-plus years old, with nearly 200,000 miles on it, but he was fond of it. He especially liked the huge V-8 engine, which he'd occasionally topped out at over 140 miles an hour. He picked up his cell and called the two officers who were on the lookout while eating their lunch in a McDonald's parking lot.

"Detective Washburn here. Ms. Krueger's headed your way, and I saw her drinking from a flask, so there's your excuse to pull her over."

The officers watched DC as her yellow Mazda flew past the McDonald's. They clocked her at 30 miles over the speed limit and swung into action, their red and blue lights flashing. George accelerated to catch up with them. He watched as DC looked in her rearview mirror and pulled over to the shoulder. The officers got out of their car and ambled over to her. George pulled up right behind them.

"Excuse me, ma'am. It looks like you were exceeding the speed limit back there," the male officer said. "Let's start with your driver's license."

DC fumbled through her purse. As she opened her wallet, she spotted the flask on the passenger seat. *Oh, shit.*

"Ms. Krueger, have you been drinking?"

"No, officer, I don't drink alcohol." Her fingers were crossed in her lap.

"Ma'am, please step out of your vehicle."

DC hesitated. *Should I just hit the gas and take off? After all, my apartment is close by, and I have underground parking. If I can just get home, I can sleep off the vodka and meet Tim in the morning.* She looked at the two officers. The female officer had her hand on the butt of her service revolver. *Maybe that's not such a good idea after all.*

DC eased herself out of her car. As the male officer took a step toward her, she doubled over and upchucked, spewing vomit all over his polished black shoes. He jumped back as the stench of vodka and puke enveloped him.

"Ms. Krueger, it would appear that you have been drinking. You're under arrest for drunken driving. Put your hands behind you. Officer, would you do the honors?"

DC held up her vomit-covered hands. The female cop shuddered and put the handcuffs back on her belt. "Never mind. Just get in the squad car." The officer gingerly placed her hands on the back of DC's shoulders while trying not to step in the puddle of puke.

George couldn't help but laugh as he watched the officers wrangle DC into the back seat of the car, slam the door, and drive away. He pulled his Impala up behind DC's Mazda. Stepping carefully around the vomit, he opened the passenger door. He reached into the pocket of his sport coat and took out a pair of thin rubber gloves and a couple of plastic bags stenciled with the word Evidence. He pulled on the gloves and placed DC's flask in a bag. He opened the glove box, took out a syringe, put it in the other bag, and went back to his car, grinning. *Much obliged, Ms. Krueger.*

17

MARY SET THREE CANS OF Diet Coke and three glasses filled with ice on the table.

"We don't need no stinkin' glasses." Omar picked up the can in his huge hand, popped the top, and took a long swig.

"Is that real?" Mary asked, pointing to his ring.

"Nah, you can pick them up on Amazon, 49 bucks, and free shipping if you're a Prime member."

"Seriously? Those diamonds look mighty real to me." Mary narrowed her eyes, a smile playing on her lips. "Whatever. Your pizzas should be up in a minute."

She stopped by the next table and chatted with three fishermen. One of them, in a Packers cap, was staring at Omar. He turned around to his buddies and whispered something. They started staring at Omar, too, with their mouths open.

A bell dinged, and two steaming pizzas landed in the pass-through window as if by magic. Omar flashed a big grin. "What the hell just happened? Did those pizzas cook themselves?"

"Nah, that's Mary's husband Robb back there," Jake said. "He makes pizza like you play football. Once upon a time, I was a venture capitalist before I became a financial advisor.

If I were still in the industry, I'd invest heavily in Robb and Mary. They're in an asset class all their own."

Mary picked up the pizzas and set them in front of Omar. She pointed at the wooden box that held the napkins and the shakers of salt, pepper, red pepper flakes, and parmesan. "Can I get you guys anything else?"

"Can I get another one of these, please?" Omar held up his empty can.

"I'd be happy to bring you another. I'll even give it to you on the house if you give me your autograph, Mr. Omar Carter, former Green Bay Packer and future NFL Hall of Famer." She laughed and clapped him on the back. "Picked up a $49 Super Bowl ring on Amazon, my ass!"

"Say, there is one more thing you can help me with," Omar said. "I'd love to find a woman as beautiful and nice as you. Got any friends?"

"Flattery will get you everywhere, Omar." Mary's cheeks were turning pink. "I actually do. My friend Laurie Lion is as sweet and charming as you. She works at Lakewoods, where Steve, one of her best customers, asks her to marry him every Friday night. It's not just for the clam chowder and fish fry. Laurie is stunning. She's tall and fit, like you. And for what it's worth, she used to be a stripper in Chicago."

"You had me at tall and fit, but stripper? Are you kidding me? That's the pepperoni on my pizza. How far is Lakewoods from here?"

"Before you head over there, you should know she's a really big Bears fan."

"Darn it, I knew it was too good to be true. But hey, for the right woman, even a leopard can change its spots."

"Yeah, right, Omar. But what are you going to do if she won't date a Packer?" Jake said.

Word spread like wildfire that there was a famous Green Bay Packer at the Loon Saloon, and, within minutes, fans were lined up all the way from the door to the far edge of the parking lot. Jake and Beth watched as Omar graciously greeted each person and signed their caps, footballs, and other Packers swag. He even signed a couple of Bears caps for some folks from Chicago. After the last fan left the saloon, Omar stood up and signaled to Mary. She hurried over and snatched the bill from his hand.

"Mr. Carter, dinner is on the house. My husband Robb and I are over the moon. You were the hit of the evening, and we appreciate the extra business from all your fans."

"Mary, the pleasure was mine." Omar scooped her up in a giant hug. "It was great to meet you, and I'm always happy to talk to Packers fans."

The crowd at the bar waved goodbye, shouting, "Go Packers!"

18

BACK IN THE CAR, JAKE DIRECTED Omar to turn left, head three miles up Pioneer Road past Charlie Best's Pioneer Bar, and then turn onto a narrow gravel road to reach the Fleischauers' cabin. John Michaud's police car was parked in front. As they stepped out into the carport, John came around the side of the cabin to greet them. "Hi, folks. Can we go out on the deck, Jake?"

"Okay, we'll be there in a minute."

"Just you, Jake. Omar and Beth Ann, you mind hanging out inside? I need to speak to Jake in private."

Jake looked at Omar and Beth Ann and shrugged. They all went into the cabin, where Jake grabbed two bottles of Spotted Cow from the fridge and went out to the deck. John was leaning over the rail, admiring the view. "Nice place you have here."

"Not mine, Chief. It belongs to the Fleischauers. They're good friends of Beth Ann and me."

"Any friend that keeps Spotted Cow on hand is a friend indeed." John took a healthy swig. "Now, my apologies for the intrusion, but I have a proposal for you. If you accept it, you can share it with Omar and Beth Ann. If not, keep it to yourself, and if you tell anyone, I'll deny everything."

Jake settled himself in a deck chair and put his feet up on the ottoman. "Well, Chief, to be honest, I've only known you for a few hours, so I have no idea what you have up your sleeve. But since you're Omar's favorite brother-in-law, I'm happy to hear what you have to say."

"Thanks, Jake. I appreciate your trust. Here's the thing. We don't get a lot of untimely deaths up here in Bayfield County. Occasionally, there are some fatal car accidents, but they're mostly tourists who don't know the roads or underestimate the deer. Unfortunately, we're also seeing an increase in suicides. Some are overdoses, either accidental or intentional, but others are a way out for folks who can't make it on Social Security alone."

"Trust me, I get it. I'm a financial advisor, and I have a number of clients who've lost most of their assets in the recession, and now they're facing retirement without a safety net. Scary stuff."

"Sure is. But in addition to the normal stuff, there have been two unsolved murders in the past 18 months. The victims were both deputies in my department and good friends of mine."

"Chief, I'm sorry to hear that. That's tough."

"You're not kidding. Now what I'm about to tell you is conjecture on my part, but I'd swear on my grandmother's grave that I'm one hundred percent right. These two guys were decent, God-fearing men and fine husbands and fathers. They were good officers, and I guess I feel responsible for their deaths."

"I understand." A loon's haunting cry echoed over the lake. "I know that feeling. It's hard, even when intellectually you know you didn't have anything to do with the murders."

"I had a feeling you'd get it. Why don't we take a little ride, and I'll give you the backstory." John handed Jake his empty bottle and belched. "That Spotted Cow tasted mighty good. Why don't you stop in the kitchen on your way out and grab a couple more?"

Jake grabbed a couple of beers and walked into the great room, where Beth Ann and Omar were playing a game called Quiglar.

"What did John have to say?" Beth Ann asked.

"Not much, except that he's got a proposal for me. We're going for a drive so he can tell me the situation."

"In a police car? With a couple of Spotted Cows?"

"Well, I guess if the chief's driving, he can't pull you over!" Omar was laughing.

"We'll wait up for you, and then you can tell us all about it," Beth Ann said.

"Maybe, maybe not," Jake said as he went out the door. "It all depends on whether I accept the proposal."

"What do you make of that?" Beth Ann asked Omar.

"Well, I've known John for nearly twenty years, and, in all that time, I've never known him to ask anybody for help. If he's got a proposal for Jake, it's serious."

▲ ▼ ▲

John drove to the lake without saying a word and pulled into the parking lot of the Cable town dump. Jake opened the beers and handed one to him. John drank deeply, staring at the mounds of garbage illuminated by the rising moon. Finally, he spoke, spitting out each word. "Orval fucking Zachariah is the biggest asshole I have ever met."

Jake just listened.

"So here's what I know. My deputy, Paul Karl, pulled Zack, as he's more commonly known, over for speeding. He was only going eight miles over the speed limit, and normally, we don't stop locals unless they're going at least twenty miles over. But Paul had a history with Zack, and he wanted to nail him for drunk driving, so he stopped him on the main street in Bayfield, in plain view of all the good citizens and tourists. Paul did everything by the book. He made Zack walk a straight line and even recite the alphabet backwards, which most people can't do, even if they're sober. Finally, Paul did a breathalyzer test, and you know what he found?"

"Let me guess. Nothing."

"Bingo. Zack was sober as a newborn baby. And, according to the onlookers, he didn't get angry. He just smiled at Paul and took the ticket. He tipped his cap, got back in his car, and drove off at five miles an hour. Two months later, they found a big pool of Paul's blood in his police car on the far side of the county. They figured whoever killed him used a long-range rifle and made off with his goddamn body, so the district attorney couldn't prosecute. 'No body, no evidence,' the D.A. said, and goddamn it, he was right."

"Brutal. You said there were two murders. What was the other one?"

"My other deputy, a guy named Taylor Sims, was killed on the anniversary of Paul's death. Damn near to the hour, and his body disappeared, too. You and I both know these aren't coincidences."

"No, they're surely not."

"Taylor was an average deputy, but he was a devout Catholic, and he left a great wife with a bun in the oven and seven cute kids under the age of ten. All he had was the little bit of life insurance the force provided him as part of his benefits. Hell, it didn't even cover his funeral. And ready for the kicker? Zack renamed two of his hogs and let everyone know. Want to know their names?"

"Let me guess. Paul and Taylor."

John nodded. He tipped the last of his beer into his mouth, staring straight ahead. John's rugged profile reminded Jake of a couple of his older clients. Proud, accomplished, and stoic, these guys had made a career of hiding their feelings. Jake understood that beneath John's tough-guy demeanor, he was racked with guilt and grief. At that moment, he made up his mind to help him find a modicum of peace.

"John, how about if we head back to the cabin?" Jake said gently. "And the answer is yes, I accept."

19

DC SAT IN HER CELL, CURSING her bad luck. A female guard had allowed her a two-minute shower before taking her mug shot and fingerprints. DC had the good sense to demand a call to Tim, but his receptionist said he was out of the office. She left a message, and the guard led her back to her cell. She was lying on her cot with her eyes closed when George materialized on the other side of the bars.

"Well, hello, Ms. Krueger. Long time no see."

If only I could kick that stupid grin off his stupid face. DC put her middle finger up in the air.

"Now, is that any way to treat an old friend?"

That guffaw of his is too fucking much. She put both middle fingers in the air.

"Now, DC, don't you know that giving the finger is *passé?* If you want to be cool, you point your finger and say the words, 'Just die.'"

DC stared at George. "Did you just say, 'Just die?'"

"Yes, I did, Ms. Krueger, and based on your response, it would appear you know exactly what I'm talking about."

DC squeezed her eyes shut, thinking about the night the momma racoon died and her last conversation with Dario, and wishing George would go away and leave her alone. When she opened them, another man's voice was coming through the bars. "Well, if it isn't George f-ing Washburn in the flesh. What the hell are you doing harassing my client?" Tim's fists were clenched, and his nose was about half an inch from George's face. "Now you leave my client alone, or I'll call foul."

George started to say something, but then shut his mouth and stomped off down the hall.

"DC, I'm going to see about getting you out of here ASAP," Tim said gently. "This is entrapment, and Gino Sweeney, George Washburn, and the entire Hopkins police force knows it. It's bullshit, and I damn well won't put up with it. Now wait here and I'll be back shortly."

DC sighed. *Bullshit is right. And boy, do I need a fix.*

Twenty minutes later, the guard returned and unlocked the door to DC's cell. "Follow me," she said as she led the way to the conference room, where Tim was talking on his cell. DC sat down, opened the bottle of water that had been provided, and listened to Tim's side of the conversation.

"Listen, Gino, this is totally bush league, and you know it," Tim was saying.

Gino said something that made Tim frown. "That's not possible. Okay, I'll talk to her, but give us half an hour before you come barging in here."

Tim hung up and opened a bottle for himself. "So, DC, how are you doing?"

"Okay, I guess, now that you're here."

"Good. I'm working on getting you out of here, but you need to tell me about the syringe that George found in your glove box."

"I don't know what you're talking about."

"Damn it, DC, don't bullshit me. I've known George for a lot of years. He may not be the greatest officer in the world, but if he tells me there was a syringe in your glove box, I believe him."

"Well, what if he planted it there, like they do on TV?"

"Oh, for Chrissakes, DC, the syringe was filled with morphine, and it had a sticker on it from your father's veterinary clinic where you just happen to work."

DC started to cry.

Tim grabbed a box of tissues from the credenza and handed it to DC. "Now listen to me, DC. You need to get a hold of yourself. The detectives are on their way, and they're going to want answers to a bunch of questions. But in the meantime, I need to know exactly what the hell is going on."

DC took a tissue, wiped her eyes, and blew her nose. "These aren't Puffs with lotion, are they?"

"DC, you are something else. You just got busted for a DUI and now you're complaining about the quality of the tissues?"

"Yeah, my father says I'm a hoot."

"That's not going to get you anywhere with Gino and George. Now start talking, and don't stop 'til you've told me everything. Remember, I'm your attorney, so whatever you say is confidential."

"Yeah, I know." DC shook her head as if to clear out some massive cobwebs and then began talking. She explained how one of her mother's paramours had hit on her when she was twelve. He plied her with liquor and drugs, and she got hooked. High school was a blur, and by the time she was in her twenties, her life revolved around drugs, liquor, and shopping. She told Tim how Dario, her supplier, was on his way to rob Jake's house when he died on the trail. She explained how she went to her dad's clinic to score some morphine and heard Beth Ann and two friends in the hallway. She took a breath, and Tim put his hand on hers.

"DC, thank you for sharing your story. Let's see about getting you out of this mess, and then, how about if we work together to get you off the drugs?"

DC looked down and nodded. There was a knock on the door.

"Ah, that must be our illustrious detectives. Let's see what they have to say. And remember, DC, I answer the questions, not you."

20

WHEN JOHN AND JAKE GOT back to the cabin, they could smell firewood burning in the night air. Jake went to the fridge and took out two bottles of Totally Naked, his other favorite brew. John was in the great room, looking at the handmade wall hangings. "Wow, this is an awesome place, not too big and not too small," John said, and took the beer. "I'd be happy to live here. Does it have heat?"

"Sure does. Alan and his wife, Paula, added central air and a good water filter, since the water up here sometimes smells like sulfur."

"Sign of the devil." John followed Jake outside to the firepit, where Beth Ann and Omar were sitting in lawn chairs, looking at the lake.

"About time you two got back. I need another glass of wine." Beth Ann raised her wine glass.

"Chief, you go sit down," Jake said. "I'll get it."

John collapsed into a chair and sighed. He looked up at the stars and said, "Boy, it's been a long time since I sat around a campfire. I'd forgotten how nice it is. Fire, water, and cold beer—it just doesn't get any better than this."

"Here you go, princess, your wish is my command." Jake handed Beth Ann a glass of chardonnay and sat down next to her. A loon yodeled in the distance. "Sounds like a male marking his territory. They say loons bring good luck."

"How can you tell it's a male, and how do you know he's marking his territory?" Omar asked as he poked the fire with a long stick.

"Loons have very distinct sounds for different circumstances," Beth Ann replied. "When they wail, they're trying to find other loons. Hooting is reserved for calling their mate and chicks. They also have a tremolo, a wavering call that means they are arriving or alarmed. And the yodel, which we just heard, is the call that males make when they're marking their territory."

"Who knew?" Omar said. "So, Jake, what did you decide?"

Jake looked at him and Beth Ann and then tipped his bottle toward the chief. "I'm going to mark my territory," he said with a wink.

"If this plays out the way I'm envisioning it, you two will be playing an important role," Jake said. "But first, I want you to hear the story straight from the horse's mouth, so to speak. Chief, tell Omar and Beth Ann what you told me."

When John finished recounting the story, Beth Ann stood up and disappeared into the darkness. She returned with an armful of firewood and fed the campfire. She sat down in her lawn chair and looked at her empty wine glass. "Gentlemen, this case calls for something stronger than beer or wine. Last time I checked, there was a bottle of 18-year-old Glenlivet in Alan's liquor cabinet. How about if we borrow it and toast the downfall of Orval Zachariah?"

Omar stood up and stretched. "My turn to wait on you, so I'll fetch it. Besides, I need to pee, as well." He returned five minutes later with the bottle of scotch, a full ice bucket, three small crystal tumblers, and a Diet Coke, which was tucked in his armpit.

Beth Ann poured a glass for Jake and another for John. The chief held up his glass so the flames from the campfire could illuminate the amber liquid. "You know what they say about scotch. The first glass is nasty, the second one is just fine, and the third is not nearly enough."

"Cheers, Chief," Jake said. "And here's to Mary Jane. Her words keep ringing in my ears, and I'm afraid she's right. Who knows how long this power will last? To that end, I'm ready to take down Orval Zachariah. Not just because he killed two good deputies but also because he decimated their families and left them without fathers and husbands to provide for them."

"Thank you, Jake. I appreciate your sense of justice," John said.

"So it sounds like Zack has a bit of a drinking problem," Jake said. "How about we follow him to his favorite watering hole and take care of him there?"

"Great idea. Tomorrow is Saturday, so I'm sure Zack will be out on the town. One of my deputies, Steve Krumrie, knows his habits, so I'll check in with him to get some intel."

"Omar, I'm going to need your help," Jake said.

"Count me in, *kemo sabe,*" Omar said, crushing his soda can in his massive fist. "Hell, I'd be happy to handle this asshole by myself. Any chance you could loan me your magical power for a night?"

"Careful what you wish for!" Jake said.

"I'm going to call Steve on my way home," John said. "I know he'll want to join us. Mind if I invite him to the party?"

"You're the Chief, so okay," Jake said. "But only Steve."

"Thanks, Jake. This means the world to me."

21

THERE WAS A KNOCK ON THE door, and Tim opened it. Gino walked in and sat down across the table from DC. George set DC's flask and syringe on the table with a flourish and took the chair next to Tim.

"So you don't do drugs, Ms. Krueger?" Gino said.

"Listen, Detective, you have absolutely no proof, other than what our friend Burnsey told you," Tim said sternly. "He claims he found that syringe in Ms. Krueger's glove box, but maybe I believe him and maybe I don't."

"Oh, he found it in her car, you can be sure of that," Gino said. "But here's the deal, Counselor. I'm not interested in busting Ms. Krueger for a DUI or even for doing drugs. I just want to know who killed Dario Q. Mohammed. But if you and Ms. Krueger will cooperate with us, we'll look the other way regarding whoever sent Dario to Jake's home. But only if you cooperate today, not tomorrow, and not the day after."

Tim looked at DC, and she nodded. "Let's do it," she whispered. "I'm sure Jake and Beth Ann are the killers."

"Okay, we're willing to cooperate," Tim said. "But we want it in writing today, with the D.A.'s signature, or there's no deal."

"We're way ahead of you, Counselor," Gino said. George pulled an envelope from the pocket of his sport coat and tossed it across the table.

Tim opened the envelope and scanned the document. He nodded at DC. "Fine. Go ahead and tell them what happened."

DC took a deep breath and plunged into her story. She came clean about her drug habit and explained how she'd met Dario, who did double duty as a dealer and burglar. When she'd heard about Jake's stroke from Beth Ann, she figured it would be an easy smash 'n' grab, figuring Jake would be in the hospital for a couple of weeks. She admitted to being on the phone with Dario when he saw Jake and Beth Ann on the deck and crashed into the oak tree. Sparing no detail, she explained how she went to the clinic to get some morphine and saw Beth Ann, Jake, and another guy in the hallway with the racoons. She'd heard Jake say the words "Just die," and then heard Beth Ann say it was the fourth time they'd killed something, with the first three times being people. She concluded her story with the phone call from the girl who'd found Dario's cell and then abruptly hung up on her. DC took another deep breath. "So that's all I know. As I'm sure you'll agree, you've got a bunch of killers on the loose."

"Thank you, Ms. Krueger," Gino said. "But we still don't know what killed Dario. There was no gunshot, and, based on the autopsy, his injuries shouldn't have been fatal."

"Maybe it was a blowgun. My father keeps them at the clinic for rabid animals, and Beth Ann knows exactly where they're stored. Maybe she shot Dario with a blowgun, which made him crash into the tree."

"Now that's a stretch," Gino said.

"I don't think it is, actually. I think I'm right. You better check it out."

▲ ▼ ▲

Omar drove through downtown Bayfield, a town that liked to imagine it invented the apple. He passed several billboards advertising the fall apple festival and countless shops selling apple pies, apple mugs, and apple tchotchkes until he reached the outskirts of town. He spotted the sign for the Don't Come Inn and pulled into an adjacent parking lot, where the Chief was waiting in an unmarked squad car, and deputy Steve Krumrie was waiting in another.

After the Chief had briefed Steve on the mission, he accepted immediately. Ever since Zack had killed Paul Karl, his best friend in the world, Steve had been on a mission from God to avenge his death, which is why he had Paul's 12-gauge shotgun with him. Steve knew everything about Zack, including the fact that the Don't Come Inn was his favorite tavern. Zack had laid claim to a seat at the horseshoe-shaped bar, which is where he announced he'd changed his hogs' names to Paul and Taylor.

"Okay, Omar, you ready for this?" Jake said.

"Are you kidding me? I haven't been so amped since my first Super Bowl." Omar reached under the seat and pulled out a SIG Sauer handgun.

"What the hell? Is that the gun that punk gangbanger dropped under your old Camry?"

"Sure is! I know you've got your plan, but as Mike Tyson once said, 'Plans are only good right up until you get punched in the face.' As I told you before, this gun gives me—and you—options. Now jump out so I can get going."

"Let's do it!" Beth Ann said. She got into the front seat of the chief's car, and Jake slid into the passenger seat. He rolled down the window and looked at Omar, who was wearing his old grass-stained Packers jersey, his newly shined Super Bowl ring, and a brand-new Packers cap.

"Go with God, buddy. I'll see you shortly," Omar said.

Jake drove over to the tavern parking lot, backed into a spot, locked the vehicle, and strode up to the entrance. Omar held the door for two bikers, who looked him up and down.

"Nice outfit," the first guy said.

"Go, Pack," the second guy said, giving him a thumbs-up.

Just as Steve had predicted, Zack was sitting at one end of the horseshoe-shaped bar with a bottle of Budweiser and a full shot glass of whiskey. Omar stepped up to the bar.

"What can I get you?" the bartender asked.

"Two ice-cold Diet Cokes and two cheeseburgers," Omar said, taking his wallet out of his back pocket.

"Your money's no good here, Mr. Omar Carter." The barkeep pointed to a framed photo of the Packers, taken right before the Super Bowl. "It's an honor to have you at the Don't Come Inn, so dinner's on the house."

"Why, thank you! What's your name?"

"It's Ben."

"Nice to meet you, Ben." Omar reached over and took a pen out of Ben's shirt pocket. He took off his Packers cap, wrote something on it, and handed it over.

Ben read aloud, "To Ben, the best bartender in the world. Your friend, Omar Carter."

"Thanks, Omar! This is really cool. My son will go crazy when he hears that I met you."

"My pleasure! And while I'm waiting on those burgers, I'm going to stop in the men's room and see a man about a horse, then settle myself in a booth."

Jake's cell phone rang, and he put it on speaker so the chief and Beth Ann could hear Omar. "Hey there. I'm in the men's room and Zack's at the bar, wearing a freakin' Vikings jersey with Tommy Kramer's name on the back. I've just ordered a couple of cheeseburgers, and I'm going to sit in a booth and sign some autographs if anybody wants one. So Jake, wait up for another 10 minutes and then come in the front."

Jake looked at Beth Ann and the chief. "It's showtime."

"Oh, Jake, are you sure you want to do this?" Beth Ann was turning pale. "It's like murder."

"I know, I thought of that. But I don't think I'd ever be convicted of anything for just pointing my finger at someone and saying a couple of words. Right, Chief?"

Ten minutes later, Jake walked into the tavern and took a seat at the farthest end of the bar, away from the cameras above the cash registers. Zack had his nose in his scotch and Omar was in a booth, signing autographs and taking selfies with Packers fans.

Ben noticed Jake and ambled over to him. "Sorry, man, didn't see you come in. What'll it be?"

"I'll take a Spotted Cow, if you have one."

"We certainly do. They're ground up in our burgers!" Ben slapped his hand on the bar and laughed at his own joke.

"*Touché.* So how about a Leinie?"

"Done. By the way, if you're a Packers fan, that is the one and only Omar Carter, future NFL Hall of Famer, over there. If you want his John Hancock, you better get in line."

"Thanks, but I'm a Bears fan." Jake crossed his fingers under the bar.

Ben shrugged. "Well, I wouldn't broadcast that in here. Be back in a moment. Got to deliver The Man his burgers."

Jake looked down the bar at Zack's ugly mug. "Hey, Zack," he said. The pig farmer set down his drink and stared back. Jake cocked his finger like a pistol and pointed it at him. "This is for Paul and Taylor. May you rot in hell."

Zack snickered.

"Just die," Jake said quietly.

Omar watched Zack's body go limp. His head smacked against the bar, knocking over his Budweiser and creating a puddle of foam around his sneering face.

Jake put a ten-dollar bill on the bar and walked out the door.

In the parking lot, Steve rolled down his window, and Jake gave him a thumbs-up.

Beth Ann got out of John's car and wrapped her arms around Jake. "Oh, honey, I hope you're okay." He hugged her tightly and nodded, not saying a word. He opened the back door and they both climbed into the back seat.

"Hey, Chief, it's done," Jake said quietly. "Now let's get the hell out of here."

The chief turned and reached for Jake's hand. "Thank you, Jake. You did a good thing for Paul and Taylor, and I'll forever owe you."

"You're welcome, John."

Jake leaned back in the seat and closed his eyes. *What would my mother say about what I just did? Would she be horrified? What would my dad think? Would he be proud of me for ridding the world of an asshole?*

A memory from high school floated into his consciousness. He was walking into his family's living room, spitting mad. His dad, Arnie, retired general counsel of Sentry Insurance, was still in his tennis clothes. He was pouring himself a scotch and soda. "How was your day, Jake?" Arnie asked. He eased himself into his recliner and took a sip. "From the look on your face, it appears you ran into one of the world's many assholes."

"I sure did. I was waiting to back into a parking spot, and he slid in before me. What a total jerk."

"Jake, my boy, how many assholes do you think are in the United States?"

That made Jake grin. "Heck, I have no idea." He always loved his father's whimsically Socratic questions.

"Take a guess."

"How about 15 percent?"

"Based on experience, I'd say your estimate is low, but for the purposes of our discussion, let's assume you're right. We've got about 25,000 people here in Stevens Point, so that means 3,750 of them are assholes. Consider yourself lucky you met only one of them today. Could have been much worse. Now make yourself a drink and take a load off your feet."

Jake laughed and helped himself to his father's scotch. "The hell with assholes!" Arnie clinked his glass with Jake's.

22

AS JOHN DROVE BACK TO THE cabin, he thought back to the first time he had killed another human being, the memory as vivid as yesterday. He was 19, in Vietnam. Out on dusk patrol with eight members of his Army squad, he was bringing up the rear. They rounded a curve in the makeshift trail when he spotted a sniper sitting near the top of a tall *Dipterocarpaceae* tree, a ubiquitous species with a shuttlecock-shaped fruit that actually spun in the air as it dropped to the ground.

The sniper was taking aim at John's sergeant, the man who'd taken him under his wing and taught him everything he knew about the jungle and the Cong. John stopped and raised his M1 30-caliber carbine, the hot jungle sweat trickling down his face and seeping into his eyes. He took aim and squeezed the trigger gently, just as his sergeant had taught him. The Viet Cong dropped from his lofty perch, twisting like a shuttlecock fruit before landing with a sickening thud at the sergeant's feet.

"You okay, John?" Beth Ann asked.

"Yeah, I was just thinking about my first kill in Vietnam. It doesn't matter whether you blow a sniper's head off at a distance or look a man in the eye and whisper 'Just die.' It's tough either way."

"You're spot-on, Chief," Jake said with a heavy sigh. "The moment I spoke those words, I knew I'd never be the same. But damn it, I'm glad I did it, and I'd do it all over again. Now let's go find that bottle of scotch and drink to Paul and Taylor."

▲ ▼ ▲

The chief parked in the Fleischauers' driveway. He turned to Jake and Beth Ann, who were holding hands in the back seat. "How about if I make us a campfire while you two lovebirds get the drinks, and we can wait for Omar." Beth Ann poured herself a glass of Chardonnay, and Jake picked up the bottle of scotch. They went out to the yard, where Jake filled glasses for John and himself.

"So, Jake, how are you doing?" John asked.

"To be honest, I don't really know. As I said, I'm glad I did it, and I'd do it again. But, I..."

"Listen, Jake, you don't have to explain. I totally get it. But even if you'd do it again, it hurts. There's something about taking somebody's life that destroys a part of your soul and makes you feel like less of a human being."

"That's exactly right, Chief. Even though I'm at peace with what I did for Paul and Taylor, I don't feel whole. It's like a piece of me is gone."

"I'm sorry to say it'll never come back. You know that saying, 'time heals everything'? Well, sad to say, it's not true if you've killed someone. Even though Zack was a flaming asshole, he was still a human being."

"Oh, John, it sounds like you're speaking from experience," Beth Ann said.

"Yes, unfortunately I am. When I was in Vietnam, I killed more than my share of Viet Cong. But I realize now that we, the United States, were the assholes in that war. The Viet Cong were just defending their territory, and that eats at me whenever I think about it."

"So, what do you do about that?" Jake asked.

"I try not to think about it."

At that moment, Omar appeared out of the darkness and sat down in a lawn chair. "My God, Jake, that was a thing of beauty. I never would have believed it if I hadn't seen it."

"What happened after I left?" Jake asked.

"If you can believe it, nobody, not even Ben the bartender, noticed Zack was dead for at least 20 minutes. As soon as Ben realized it, he told the owner, and they moved him from the bar to a booth."

"Did anyone call the police?" John asked.

"No need. Deputy Steve Krumrie just happened to stop by, so he helped them prop him up and bought everyone a drink. The owner started singing 'Ding dong, the Zack is dead,' and everyone joined in. It was nuts!"

"Okay, that makes me feel so much better," Jake said.

"Yeah, you guys would have loved it. I really wanted to stay and party with all my new friends, but I knew you were waiting for the report. Before I left, Steve told me they were going to put Zack in his car at closing time, so it looked like he died behind the wheel. You know, Zack must have been one sorry human being. I've never heard so many fuck yous tossed around since we last played the Bears. So kudos to you, Jake. You did great, and I'm proud to call you my friend."

"Thank you, Omar. I appreciate that."

"Jake, Zack was a wicked man, plain and simple," Beth Ann said. "And God bless you for purging an evil human being from this Earth. I know God has reserved a special spot in heaven just for you!"

"Right next to Vince Lombardi's house!" the chief said.

▲ ▼ ▲

After the chief finished his drink and went home, Omar and Beth Ann also called it a day, leaving Jake alone with another glass of scotch. The mournful sound of loons echoed over the moonlit water. Jake thought through all the monikers for a group of loons. There was a cry of loons, a raft, a water dance, an asylum, and his favorite, a loomery of loons. It made him think about all the crazy things that had happened to him in the last couple of months.

Up until his stroke, his life had been pretty good. A natural athlete, he was on the high school wrestling team and, when he was a senior, he was runner-up in the state championship. After graduation, he spent the summer playing golf and mowing lawns before heading south to the University of Wisconsin–Madison. He joined a frat, majored in marketing, and worked part-time as a waiter at an Italian restaurant and as a bartender at a disco called Mr. Luck's.

After college, Jake moved to Minneapolis with a couple of frat buddies. They found a house in Uptown, and he took a job at a financial services firm, where he quickly discovered he was a natural advisor. Unlike many of his colleagues, he viewed his clients as humans, not merely transactions, so he never sold them an insurance product they didn't need. As a result of his charm and integrity, he quickly became a top producer, and when his boss encouraged him to get a master's degree in financial services, he readily agreed.

Over the next five years, he added numerous designations to his business card, including the coveted Certified Financial Planner, and, when he was 32, he opened his own financial services firm. As its president and as a fiduciary, he had only two cardinal rules: work only with only nontoxic clients, and do only what's best for them. As a result, his firm grew quickly, and, within three years, one of his competitors made him an offer he couldn't refuse. Which, in hindsight, was fortuitous, in light of his newly acquired power. If I were still a fiduciary, there'd be no way I could kill people, even if they were toxic.

23

TIM AND DC WALKED OUT to their cars. "Thanks for coming to my rescue, Tim," DC said. "I really appreciate it."

"Well, DC, it's all part of the service. But we need to meet again first thing tomorrow and review our strategy and next steps."

"That would be wonderful! How about lunch?"

"Okay. Noon at Jimmy's on Shady Oak Road."

DC drove directly to the clinic and chatted with her colleagues for a few minutes. Then she went down the hall, opened the storage closet, and grabbed a pair of rubber gloves. She put on a glove, then rummaged around for a blowgun dart and put it in her purse. She slipped out the back door, drove straight to Victoria, and parked near the entrance to the bike path. Walking toward Jake's house, she recognized the oak tree with the scars from Dario's accident. She put the glove back on and dropped the dart into the brush on the side of the path.

Audrey Hanes was watching from her bedroom window. *I wonder what that lady is doing?*

▲ ▼ ▲

DC drove home and took a long shower, hoping the hot water would wash away the last 48 hours. She put on a pair of sweatpants and a Bangles T-shirt and walked into the kitchen. She opened the fridge and frowned at the shelves, which held only a bottle of Famous Dave's barbecue sauce, half a carton of eggs, and half a bottle of Cosmopolitan mix.

In the living room, she flopped down on the sofa. She pulled out one of the morphine syringes from her purse and stared at it. Telling Tim and the detectives about her drug habit had been scary but cathartic. In her heart of hearts, she knew she'd needed help for a long time; otherwise, she was going to end up dead, either from suicide or an overdose. *Was Dario's death a sign from God that I should quit?*

Mustering up all her strength, she got up from the sofa, put the syringe in a drawer, and went back into the kitchen. She opened the liquor cabinet and took out a bottle of Grey Goose and a smaller bottle of triple sec. The hell with the goddamn drugs. I'm making myself a Cosmo.

▲ ▼ ▲

The next morning, George Washburn left his house early and drove out to Victoria. He parked near the bike path, got out of his car, and shuffled through the tall grass over to the tree where Dario had crashed. Near Jake's house, he spotted a tranquilizer gun dart on the ground. He bent down to pick it up and looked up at Jake's deck. *Gotcha!* He raced back to his car and slipped the dart into a plastic bag.

George walked into the Minnetonka police station with a broad grin on his face. Gino's door was closed, so he knocked. "Enter!" Gino bellowed. He was on the phone, so George parked himself in a chair and gazed around the office. The walls were covered with framed photos, mostly of Gino's beautiful red-headed wife and their four children.

George sighed as he thought about Gino's impending divorce. For the last decade, the man had been married to his job, since his only goal in life was to become the Minnetonka police chief. He got up at 5 a.m., hit the gym, and was at his desk by 7 a.m. Most days, he didn't get home until 9 or 10 p.m. Initially, Gino's wife suspected him of having a mistress on the side, so she hired a private detective from St. Paul to tail him. When he reported that her husband was doing nothing but pursuing the captain's badge, she served him with divorce papers.

Gino hung up and looked at George. "Burnsey, I was just talking to our guy at the Minneapolis morgue. They've already cremated Dario Mohammed, which is going to put a crimp in our investigation. I need you to head out to Victoria right away. I've sent out a couple of guys to look for a blowgun dart, and maybe you can help them. I know it's a long shot, but it's all we have."

"I'm way ahead of you, partner." George tossed the plastic bag onto Gino's desk.

Gino picked up the bag and frowned. "Wait, where did you get this?"

"It was on the side of the bike path behind Jake Silver's house, where your guys are probably looking as we speak."

"Holy shit, Burnsey! What the hell were you thinking? You know damn well we have a team of specialists who are paid to investigate crime scenes. Son of a bitch, why didn't you just give them a heads-up so they could have photographed the spot and measured the distance to the tree where Dario Mohammed died? For Chrissakes, your half-assed explanation of 'I found it on the bike path' is not going to cut it in court."

"I'm sorry." George hung his head. "I was just so excited that I found it, and I thought you'd want to know right away. If you want, I could take it back out to the site and show the investigators where I found it."

"No way. That wouldn't be good for either of us. Here's what we're going to do. First, I'm calling the D.A. to get a warrant out for Mr. Jake Silver. Then, based on everything that Ms. Krueger has told us about Jake and his buddies, there should be at least two more dead bodies floating around, so your job is to find them."

George waited while Gino called the D.A., who authorized them to arrest Jake and offered to find a judge to approve a search warrant for his home. Gino gave George the thumbs-up. George brightened. "Swell! How about Beth Ann Noble and Omar Carter?"

"Not yet. We'll get to them later, which will make a lot of Vikings fans very happy."

▲ ▼ ▲

Later that afternoon, Jake, Beth Ann, and Omar were sitting on the deck watching the Minnesota Twins game. When the doorbell rang, Omar opened the front door to find Gino and George on the front step. Three squad cars—two from Victoria and one from Minnetonka—were parked in front of the house. Omar shouted, "Hey, Jake, your two favorite private eyes are back again, and this time, they've brought a small army."

Jake and Beth Ann got up and joined Omar in the foyer. Jake's face was grim. "Hello, detectives. What brings you back to Victoria?"

"Mr. Silver, we're here to arrest you for the murder of Dario Q. Mohammed," Gino said, holding up the search warrant. "You have the right to remain silent. Anything you say can and will be used against you in a court of law. You have the right to an attorney. If you cannot afford an attorney, one will be provided for you. Now turn around so we can cuff you."

"Are you two out of your minds? This is outrageous!" Beth Ann shrieked. She snatched the warrant out of Gino's hand.

"Listen, Miss Noble, just be glad you're not getting arrested too. But don't worry, your time will come. Now do us a favor and stay out of the way so our officers can search the house." Gino looked at Jake and snarled, "Jake Silver, your killing days are over." He snapped the handcuffs on

Jake's wrists, and George led him out to one of the waiting squads. Omar and Beth Ann followed behind.

"Beth Ann, do me a favor and call my dad, okay?" Jake said quietly, as Gino shoved him into the back seat and slammed the door.

24

DC WOKE UP ON THE SOFA with the queen of all hangovers. She stretched her aching limbs and looked around the living room. She could remember finishing a second Cosmopolitan, but based on the empty Grey Goose bottle on the coffee table, maybe she'd had a third. She stood up, and her toes nudged a hard object. When she realized it was an empty syringe, her eyes welled up with tears and her stomach heaved.

As the bile rose in her throat, she ran to the bathroom, leaned over the toilet, and retched until there was nothing left. She wiped her mouth with a piece of toilet paper, stumbled back into the living room, collapsed on the sofa, and started sobbing. She picked up her cell phone and called her father.

He answered on the first ring. "Hey, Princess, are you okay? You didn't show up for work, so I was just about to call you."

"No, Dad, I'm not okay. I feel like hell, and I think I need to go to rehab."

"Listen, honey, I love you, and I'll get you all the help you need. Where are you right now?"

"On my sofa," she wailed.

"Okay, Princess. Just stay right where you are. I'm coming to pick you up, and we'll get you into rehab this afternoon."

"Thank you, Daddy," she said, dissolving into a fresh storm of sobs.

▲ ▼ ▲

Omar and Beth Ann went back into the house. One officer was in the living room, ripping apart the sofa cushions, and another was in Jake's office. They could hear him turning on the computer and opening file drawers, so they went out to the deck. Beth Ann called Arnie Silver and told him that Jake needed an attorney. Without asking any questions, Arnie promised to call Seth Morton, founding partner of Briggs & Morton and the best damn defense attorney in Minnesota.

Five minutes later, her phone rang. "Beth Ann Noble, this is Seth Morton," a man said in a gruff but kind voice. "I just spoke with our mutual friend Arnie Silver, and I understand his son Jake is in need of my services."

"Oh, Seth, thank you for calling." Beth Ann burst into tears. "This whole thing is so scary, and I have no idea what's happening. All I know is Jake really needs your help."

"I'm on it. Let me make some calls, and I'll be in touch. In the meantime, make sure you document everything with photos."

"Yes, thank you, Seth. I'll be sure to do that."

"Ms. Noble, we're finished for today," one of the officers called, so Beth Ann and Omar went inside the house. The two officers were standing in the living room. They had nothing in their hands, so Omar surmised they hadn't found anything.

"Now that you've torn the house apart, I trust you found what you were looking for." Omar held the front door open. The officers didn't reply as they strode out to their car and peeled out of the cul-de-sac. Omar put his arm around Beth Ann. "Listen, if it's okay with you, I'd like to call the chief."

"Oh, Omar, yes, please do! We need all the help we can get. While you do that, I'm going to take photos of every room. Seth Morton says we need to document everything."

She started in the kitchen, where she could hear Omar on his cell phone talking to his sister. "Hey there, Mary Jane. I need to talk to the chief, but I don't have his number. The goddamn Minnetonka police have arrested Jake, and I need his help, pronto."

"Done and done. I'm texting John's contact info to you as we speak. We're indebted to Jake, so just let me know if there's anything we can do."

"Sure thing, sis. I appreciate your offer. I'll explain when I can."

"No worries, little brother. You don't have to explain anything. After everything Jake's done for us, we consider him and Beth Ann part of our family. We're happy to help, no questions asked."

"Thanks, sis. I'll be in touch."

Omar hung up and dialed John's cell phone. "Michaud here, who's this?" the chief said in a gruff voice.

"Hi, Chief, it's Omar. I'm calling about Jake. He needs your help."

"What happened?"

"A bunch of detectives and cops showed up at Jake's house this morning with warrants. After going through the house from top to bottom, they arrested Jake and took him away in a squad car. Before they left, one of the detectives said they'd be coming back for Beth Ann and me."

"What the hell happened?"

"Well, assuming those cops just installed microphones in every room of Jake's house, I'd rather tell you the whole story in person. But suffice it to say, Jake's under arrest for killing a guy named Dario Q. Mohammed. As one of the detectives was cuffing Jake, he said, 'Your killing days are over.'"

"This is nuts. How can I help?"

"I'm not sure. I was hoping you'd have the answer."

"Well, I've actually been thinking quite a bit about Jake. With your approval, I'd like to talk to a friend of mine."

"Approved. Thank you, Chief."

"Omar, it's the least I can do. You take care of Beth Ann, and I'll report back."

John hung up and called Ted Janick, his sergeant from Vietnam. The call went immediately to voicemail. *This is Ted. I am either out on my boat, or wishing I was. You know what to do at the beep.*

"It's John. Get off your goddamn boat and call me back. I need your help." John sat back in his chair, knowing Ted would call back as fast as possible. Even though they never spoke of the time John saved Ted's life, the experience had cemented a deep friendship that both men treasured, even if several months went by between conversations.

John knew that Ted had one son who'd followed in his footsteps. Ted Jr., known as TJ, was about Jake's age. A former Coast Guard officer, TJ had been promoted after 9/11 to senior level officer in the Federal Protective Service in the Department of Homeland Security, otherwise known as DHS. John knew the DHS could overrule damn near any law enforcement agency, including the pissant Minnetonka police department. He also knew that the DHS would be able to use Jake's powers for the good of the country.

25

SETH MORTON, ATTORNEY at Law, reached into the pocket of his suitcoat and pulled out a crumpled pack of unfiltered Camels along with a silver lighter bearing the head of a bulldog that Jake recognized as a Dunhill. It must have cost at least $700, but since Seth's nickname was Bulldog, it was worth every penny.

Seth shook out a cigarette, lit it, took a long drag, and sighed. "God, that's good."

Jake grimaced. "Seth, with all due respect, I'm pretty sure there's no smoking in here."

"Yeah, so what?" Seth replied. "Let 'em sue me." He took another deep drag of the cigarette and coughed. He opened the front flap of his suitcoat, revealing a shoulder holster with a snub-nosed revolver. "Or I could just kill anybody who objects. Listen, don't worry about me, Jake. I have only three vices—smoking, drinking expensive scotch, and eating double cheeseburgers, especially from the Lion's Tap—and I enjoy all of them. I don't give a damn if they kill me, since none of us are getting out of here alive."

Jake reached for the pack of cigarettes, took one out, and sniffed it. "God, my old man used to smoke these a long time ago."

"He still does, Jake my boy, just not when you or your mother are around." Seth laughed, which made him cough again. "Now put my cigarette back in the pack and tell me why the hell you're being charged with murder."

Jake launched into his story and Seth listened intently, puffing on his cigarette. When Jake was finished, Seth lit another cigarette and walked over to the window. He pointed at a woman pushing a stroller on the sidewalk. "So, you're telling me that you could just point your finger at that woman and whisper, 'Just die,' and then she'd keel over?"

"I'm afraid so."

"Well, if you weren't Arnold Silver's son, I'd say this is part of some elaborate scam or crazy reality show. But goddamn it, neither your dad nor your mom raised you to be a liar. So, Jake, if you say this is so, then, by God, I believe you."

"Thank you, Seth," Jake said in a near-whisper. "So, if I have the ability to simply point my finger and kill someone, I would have no reason to use a blowgun dart, right?"

▲ ▼ ▲

Chief John Michaud looked at the huge pile of paperwork on his desk, wishing he could point his finger and make it all go away. He had just finished skimming and signing the last document when his cell phone rang. It was Ted Janick, his Nam buddy.

"Hello, my friend, how are you?" John said.

"I'm hunky and dory, simultaneously. And how the heck are you?"

"Better than I've ever been. Orval Zachariah is no longer walking the Earth, so I can finally rest easy, knowing the man who murdered my two deputies is rotting in hell."

"Cheers to you. Without bodies or evidence, that's miraculous. And since saving my life in the jungle was your first miracle, you're now two for two."

"I wish I could take credit for it, but Zack's death was not my miracle. Which is what I wanted to talk to you about."

"I'm all ears. I'm sitting on my boat with a cold beer in my hand and docked, so I'm not going anywhere."

John explained how he'd met Jake and Beth Ann at Mary Jane's cabin, and how he stood on her deck watching as Jake pointed his finger and killed a gang of marauding coyotes. He described how Jake had agreed to use his powers to eliminate Zack and avenge the deputies' deaths.

When John was finished, Ted exhaled. "Well, John, you and I have both have seen some mighty strange things in our lifetime, right? Remember those ghosts we saw in Vietnam at that spooky bar in Hanoi? And that Viet Cong with two faces and one body? Hell, even TJ swears he saw a mermaid when he was in the Coast Guard. Between you and me, I'm pretty sure there was some liquor involved with that sighting. But all kidding aside, if you say Jake's powers are genuine, I believe you. I just wish TJ were here with me, since I know he'd be interested in this."

"Thanks, Ted. As always, you and I are on the same page. I'd love to share this with TJ, since my gut says it could be used for a greater good than just killing coyotes and nasty pig farmers."

"Absolutely! I'll call him as soon as we hang up. As you and I know, he's charged with protecting America at any and all costs. You'll need to figure out how to demonstrate Jake's powers to him, of course. If you can do that, I have no doubt he'll take it all the way up to the President."

"As in POTUS? Are you serious?"

"As serious as I've ever been, pal. You can expect a call from TJ tomorrow."

The next morning, TJ Janick punched John's cell number on his desk phone and pressed record.

"Hello there, Junior! Long time no see," John said.

TJ grinned at the nickname. His father had a handful of cronies that he played poker with every Thursday night. Ted grew up calling them all "Uncle," and in return, they called him "Junior," slipping him nickels whenever they won.

"Hello, Uncle John! Or should I call you Chief Uncle John?"

"How about I call you TJ and you call me John? That is, if you're still speaking to me after this call."

"Sounds good. TJ and John it is. Based on what my father told me last night, Chief—I mean John—you've got quite an interesting tale to tell."

"I'm not sure how much your father told you, so how about if you turn off that recorder you've got going and I'll start from the beginning."

TJ laughed. *Holy smokes! I almost forgot who I was dealing with.* "Okay, John, I just turned it off. This is just between you and me." He sat back in his chair, kicked his feet up on his desk, and listened to John's story while scribbling notes.

"And there you have it." John said. "As I mentioned earlier, I wouldn't have believed it if I hadn't seen it with my own two eyes."

TJ cleared his throat, wishing he had recorded the story. "All I can say is, wow. John, if this is really true—and please understand that I'm not questioning your judgment—we may have an opportunity to help Jake and keep the American people safer than they've ever been since before 9/11."

"Junior, I mean TJ, I personally can't speak to what this means for the American people. That's way over my pay grade, which is where you come in. This is exciting, but I do want to remind you that Jake doesn't know that I'm talking to you. If and when he finds out, he may not be pleased. Hell, he may refuse to cooperate and even call me a liar."

"Yes, John, Jake could certainly do that. He could also just point his finger at you and say, 'Just die.' But from what you've told me, I'll go out on a limb and say he won't. He sounds like a solid citizen and a patriot, and, if indeed the good Lord has bestowed this wonderful power upon him, I would imagine he'd be willing to use it for the good of America. Hell, the good of the world, for that matter."

"From your mouth to God's ears," John said quietly.

"I'm intrigued, but as you well know, I need to tread lightly. If this turns out to be some elaborate hoax, my career will be over and I'll be asking you if you want fries with your Big Mac."

"Yes, TJ, that's definitely a possibility. But, on the other hand, if you can be the hero that America's been looking for since 9/11, you'll be set for life."

TJ laughed. "And now it's my turn to say, 'from your mouth to God's ears.' So here's what I'd like to do. First, I want to meet Omar, since he was in the bar when Jake told Zack to just die. I need to hear firsthand what he saw—and didn't see. I'd also like to meet Jake and his fiancée and the other cast of characters."

"Sounds like you need a trip to the great Midwest."

"My thoughts exactly. I'll tell my boss I'm taking a long overdue vacation."

"Bring your appetite. Between the beer and the pizza, we'll treat you right."

26

WHEN THE SQUAD CAR ARRIVED at the Minnetonka police station, an officer was waiting for Jake. He led him to an interrogation room with a small table, two chairs, a one-way window, and a camera in the corner. He directed Jake to sit in one of the chairs, then removed his handcuffs. He reshackled Jake's hands through a metal loop on the table, secured his feet through a loop in the concrete floor, and left the room.

Having read his share of crime novels, Jake expected a long wait and a ninth-degree interrogation. To his surprise, when the door opened, Gino and George were standing there. Gino sat down opposite Jake, and George leaned against the wall with his arms folded over his chest.

"Well, Jake, I think I've finally figured this out," Gino said proudly.

"Figured what out?" Jake whispered.

"All of this 'Just die' crap and how you used a blowgun to kill good old Dario Mohammed."

Jake's mind started doing backflips, wondering how Gino knew about his special power. "Did you say just say blowgun? That's the most ludicrous thing I've ever heard."

"Yes, I said blowgun," Gino sneered. "We found a dart from a blowgun on the bike path right below your deck. It would appear that you or your fiancée shot Dario as he was about to rob your home. We also have information on two other murders that we believe you may have committed."

He can't be talking about Orval Zachariah. That's not possible.

"My officers are looking for the blowgun in your lovely home as we speak. Once they find it, they'll arrest Beth Ann Noble and that washed-up Packer you've been running around with."

"Holy shit, Detective, you've lost your marbles."

There was a loud knock on the door. George looked at Gino and nodded. Gino reached out to turn the knob, but the door was already swinging open. A short, burly man with gray hair stepped into the room and filled it with his presence.

"Well, hello there, Jake," Seth Morton said as he put one hand on Jake's shoulder. "I haven't seen you since you were knee-high to a grasshopper. Your dad instructed me to get you out of this mess, so here I am." Seth turned to Gino and George, grinning. "Detectives, my name is Seth Morton of Briggs and Morton. It's a small firm, so you may or may not have heard of us." He pointed at the camera. "I'm going to need some private time with my client, and this room will not do at all. I'd appreciate it if you'd find us a nice conference room with some windows, a couple bottles of cold water, and two cups of fresh coffee with cream and sugar. I'd also like you to take these barbaric shackles off my friend and client, posthaste."

Gino scowled. "Fine, Morton, play it that way. George will get an officer to unlock Mr. Silver, and then he'll take you to a conference room. There's a vending machine in the hallway with water and coffee. Serve yourself."

▲ ▼ ▲

Ten minutes later, the conference room door opened and Gino and George walked in, smirking. Both men were carrying cups of steaming coffee. George set his cup on the table and took the plastic bag containing the dart out of his pocket. He tossed it on the table next to Seth's Camels. He looked longingly at the pack, but said, "Hey, Counselor, don't you know better than to smoke in here?"

"Yeah, Burnsey! So why don't you sue me?" Seth reached for another cigarette and lit it. "I know damn well that half the cops smoke on the premises, so don't bullshit me. In fact, why don't you go ahead and help yourself? If I remember correctly, you smoke like a chimney."

"No, George, you may not join our esteemed counselor in his cancer-causing habit," Gino said. "Now crack the window so we can all breathe and get down to business."

Seth exhaled a cloud of smoke, pointed at the plastic bag, and laughed. "So tell me, are you charging my client Mr. Silver with murder, based on a fucking blowgun dart?"

"Absolutely." Gino nodded while trying to bat the smoke away. "In addition to the dart, we have a witness who overheard Mr. Silver and Ms. Noble basically confess to killing two other people."

Jake opened his mouth to respond, but Seth cut him off. "Oh, for Chrissakes, Gino, this is not up to your standards. One dart and the possibility of two more murders? Really? So where are the bodies, Detective? And where did you find this dart?"

"I'll tell you exactly where we found it, Counselor. It was on the bike path right behind Jake's home. And by the way, we do have at least one body—Dario Q. Mohammed's— which was found less than 20 yards from this dart." He reached over, grabbed Seth's smoldering cigarette, and dropped it into his coffee cup, where it hissed and sizzled. "Oh, and by the way, guess who Mr. Mohammed was arguing with when he died? That's right, Jake Silver and his soon-to-be incarcerated fiancée."

Jake shook his head vehemently and started to speak, but Seth shushed him again.

"Oh, yes, Jake, we know all about your special 'Just die' code words and how you kill people with darts that Beth Ann steals from the Krueger veterinary clinic where she works," Gino continued. "Don't worry, we'll find the other bodies too, and I'm willing to bet that every one of them will have dart wounds in them."

Seth put his elbows on the table, cupped his chin in his hands, and looked into the detective's eyes. "Gino, Gino, Gino," he said with a sigh. "How long have I known you? Twenty-five years? This is a stretch, even for you, and you know it. This meeting is finished, and we'll see you in court. I look forward to getting this frivolous charge thrown out." He lit another cigarette and exhaled, then pushed the pack over to George. "You take 'em, Burnsey. It must be tough to afford them on your salary."

27

DR. WILLIAM WAS DRIVING DC TO Center City. "I need lots of help, Daddy," she said.

He reached over and put his hand on her shoulder. "And we'll get you all the help you need, Princess. However long it takes and whatever it costs, we'll solve whatever's hurting you. You're the most important person in the world to me, and I'll always be here for you."

He pulled up beneath the wide portico. A young man came out and opened the car door for DC. He extended his hand and smiled. "Welcome to Hazelden."

"You go ahead, DC," Dr William said. "I'll park the car and bring your suitcase."

The young man led DC into the foyer and through a pair of rustic wooden doors that looked as though they had once graced an old European church. She found herself in a lobby with a polished mahogany desk, a Persian rug, and photographs of beautiful lakes in all four seasons.

A woman in a white lab coat extended her hand and smiled. "Hello, Ms. Krueger, I'm Dr. Maylene de Castro. Let's go into my office so we can get acquainted while we wait for your dad." She led DC down a hallway to a door with a brass plaque with her name engraved on it. The room was spacious, with creamy white walls, a pretty desk, a sofa, and a pair of ivory leather chairs. She directed DC to sit on the sofa, and she took one of the chairs.

"So, Ms. Krueger, welcome to Hazelden. I'm very glad you're here, and I look forward to getting to know you. If you'd like, you can call me Maylene, since we generally use first names here."

DC looked down at her lap. After a moment, she looked up and took a deep breath. "Okay, thanks, I guess you can call me DC."

"If you don't mind me asking, what does DC stand for?"

DC grinned. "District of Columbia, since apparently that's where I was conceived. But no one ever calls me that. So, Maylene, what's next?"

"As soon as your father gets here, I'll show you to your room so he can help you unpack and get settled. One of our staff will stop by to explain the rules, which include no cell phones, no computers, and no drugs or alcohol, of course. Starting tomorrow morning, you'll be able to participate in both individual and group sessions. I think you'll find the group sessions very useful, since you'll quickly discover that you're not the only one dealing with addiction."

"Is that it?"

"Yes, that's basically it. It's important to remember that you're not a prisoner here. You may ask me to call your dad and he can pick you up at any time. But I would encourage you to stick it out, since you're a bright young woman and you have your whole life ahead of you."

DC sighed. "All right, I'll give it a try."

▲ ▼ ▲

The flight to Minneapolis-St. Paul International Airport was uneventful. TJ tried to sleep, but he couldn't stop thinking about his conversation with John. He knew it was only a matter of time before another 9/11—only infinitely worse—happened to his beloved America. That's why he worked such long hours, doing his best to prevent it from happening on his watch. The possibility that Jake Silver could help him was intriguing, and he was anxious to find out if his power could be harnessed for good.

When TJ told his boss he wanted to take a week's vacation in Minnesota, Da Boss, as TJ called him, immediately gave him two weeks off. "It's about time you took a break. Now here are your marching orders. Turn off your phone, don't check your email, and bring me back a case of Spotted Cow."

"Spotted what?"

"Spotted Cow. Best goddamn beer I've ever tasted," Da Boss said with a laugh.

A former Navy Seal, Da Boss had joined the CIA after his naval enlistment ran out, and he rose through the ranks to lead the Office of Countering Weapons of Mass Destruction. He spoke five languages fluently, including

Farsi, and he was dark-skinned, so people often thought he was Middle Eastern, which he used to his advantage.

Da Boss considered TJ his right-hand man. Unlike the other senior members of the division, who were merely paper pushers with MBAs from Wharton and Harvard, TJ had earned his stripes in the Coast Guard by capturing drug smugglers and wrangling tax evaders. He was passionate, dedicated, and married to his job. While he liked women very much, 9/11 had affected him deeply, and he rarely dated, preferring to bury himself in his work.

When the plane landed, TJ turned on his phone. He had a text from John informing him he was parked outside baggage claim, so he headed to the curb.

John got out of his car and gave him a big hug.

"Hey, Uncle John, long time no see!"

"Good to see you, TJ. My God, have you grown up! Hell, you look just like your old man in his younger days."

"That's what they tell me." TJ put his suitcase in the trunk and got into the passenger seat.

"First things first," John said. "We're going out to Victoria to meet Omar at Jake's house, where he's been staying while Jake's in jail."

"How much have you told Omar?" TJ asked.

"Not much. Just that you're more powerful than Vince Lombardi in his day."

▲ ▼ ▲

Omar opened Jake's front door to welcome the men. "Hey, Chief, glad you made it."

"Omar Carter, meet TJ Janick. TJ, meet Omar," John said. They shook hands and Omar led them into the kitchen.

"Very nice!" TJ said. "I'd kill to have a kitchen like this, not that I'd actually use it."

Omar opened the fridge, grabbed bottles of water and Diet Coke, and beckoned the men to follow him out to the deck. "TJ, thanks again for coming out to Minnesota. The chief said that you might be able to help Jake, but, beyond that, he hasn't told me anything about you."

TJ opened his sport coat, revealing a shoulder holster under his left armpit. He removed his wallet and handed it to Omar. He flipped it open, and his eyes widened as he looked at the shiny golden badge, inscribed with the words Department of Homeland Security and Special Agent.

"Boy, Chief, you weren't kidding." Omar handed the badge back to TJ. "This trumps Vince Lombardi's authority by a long shot."

"First of all, Mr. Carter, I'm a big fan of yours, even though I'm a dyed-in-the-wool Vikings fan," TJ said with a smile. "But as much as I enjoy talking about football, I'd rather talk about your friend Jake Silver."

"Well, TJ, the chief has vouched for you, so I'll tell you what I know in the hopes that you can get Jake out of this mess. Omar walked to the railing and pointed at the bike path. "This is where it started." He explained the series of strange occurrences and concluded with a description of the evening at the Don't Come Inn.

"I watched Jake point his finger at that goddamn hog farmer who killed John's deputies. I heard him tell Zack to just die, and that's exactly what happened. Zack slumped forward, his head hit his beer bottle and knocked it over, and he was gone, dead as can be. No blowguns, no darts, just a pointed finger and a couple of words. I swear on my grandmother's grave it happened exactly as I described it."

TJ looked at John. "All right, Chief, now I'm really intrigued. "Omar, did I see a beer in that fridge? Now that I'm officially on vacation, I could use a cold one.

"Coming right up," Omar said. He went back into the kitchen and returned with two bottles of Spotted Cow and a couple more Diet Cokes. He handed the beers to TJ, and John opened a Diet Coke.

"Spotted Cow!" TJ exclaimed. "This is my boss's favorite beer. He's given me orders to bring him back a case."

"We can certainly help you with that," John said. "Hell, with your privileges, you could fill a whole plane!"

"True that." TJ laughed, opened the bottle, and took a swig. "Shit, Da Boss is right. This is a damn good beer."

Beth Ann appeared in the doorway, grinning. "What the hell? Jake's in jail and you all are having a goddamn party! Good thing I showed up before the dancing girls arrived." She flopped into a chair and grabbed a Diet Coke.

"Beth Ann, mind your goddamn manners! We have guests here," Omar said.

"Listen, I can swear if I want to. The goddamn police were in my apartment all morning looking for a goddamn dart and a blowgun. They obviously didn't find anything, but they told me that when they find them, they're going to charge me with murder." She burst into tears, spitting out her Diet Coke. Omar went into the kitchen and brought back a box of Kleenex. She blew her nose and looked at John and TJ. "I'm so sorry. Let's start again. Hi, John. And you must be TJ."

"Hi, Beth Ann," TJ said. "As I'm sure John has told you, I'm here to see if I can help you and Jake." He opened his jacket and flashed his holstered revolver. "After what my new favorite Packer has told me about your predicament, I believe I'm the right guy for the job."

28

AT FIVE O'CLOCK, GEORGE GOT into his old Impala and tossed the plastic bag containing DC's morphine syringe onto the passenger seat. He lit one of Seth's Camels and sped home. The day hadn't gone well, and he was craving a beer. He wished there were something better in his fridge than Heineken, but his credit cards were maxed out, and he was down to drinking the cheapest beer he could tolerate.

The meeting with Seth had not gone the way he expected, and the search of Jake's home had turned up nothing. No high-tech blowguns, no dart, nothing. The D.A. was working on a search warrant for Beth Ann Noble's apartment, but George didn't hold out much hope for that. He leaned over to stub out the precious Camel in the car's ashtray, and he cursed to himself when his beer belly got in the way.

He glanced over at the plastic bag. He'd never tried morphine, or heroin, for that matter, but after looking at DC's skinny body, he thought it could be worth a try. He pulled into his cluttered one-car garage, snatched the bag, and beelined it to the kitchen.

Smiling with anticipation, he dropped the bag and his car keys on the counter and opened the old refrigerator. His smile quickly turned to a frown as he realized the Heineken carton was empty. He slammed the door and picked up his car keys. He thought about heading to his favorite gas station but stopped, thinking of his credit cards. He pulled out his wallet, hoping to find enough money for a six-pack, but the only bills were a single dollar and some pesos from a long-ago spring break in Cabo San Lucas.

He picked up a half-empty jar of coins that was sitting on the counter. He considered counting out enough quarters for the beer, but his ego got the best of him. He groaned and put the jar back on the counter, knocking the plastic bag to the floor. He sighed and bent over, cursing his beer gut yet again, and picked up the bag. Thankfully, the syringe wasn't broken. He started to set it on the counter but hesitated. He held it up to the light, admiring the amber liquid.

He set the bag on the counter, pulled out his cell phone, and googled how to use a syringe. Easy-peasy. He carried the syringe into the living room, sat down on the stained sofa, took off his sport coat, and rolled up his sleeve. He picked out a vein, pushed the needle into it, and waited. And waited. And then, he smiled.

▲ ▼ ▲

After a teary farewell with her father, DC settled into her room at Hazelden, where she had chosen to eat dinner. There was a knock on her door. It was Lawrence, the good-looking young man who'd greeted her when she arrived. He had hazel eyes and a peaceful aura.

"Hi again! I hope you're settling in." He set the tray on the desk. "The food here is pretty good, and I picked out what I thought you might like. There's a nice salad, some baked chicken, wild rice pilaf, and broccoli. And for dessert, I chose a big slice of key lime pie, my favorite."

He handed her a paper bag. She took it tentatively and looked inside. It contained several books. The first was a Bible, so she quickly put it aside and pulled out the other two. "Oh, I love Lee Child! Reacher is such a stud."

"Yeah, he's totally a stud. It's a little violent, but I appreciate the way he helps people out of some nasty jams."

She held up the next book, *Dark of the Moon* by John Sanford. "Thank you, Lawrence! I've always wanted to read his books."

"This is the first one in Sanford's Virgil Flower series. I love these books because, even though Virgil's a cop, he doesn't carry a gun. Now, your first session is at 8 a.m. tomorrow, so I hope you can get a good night's sleep." He pointed at a buzzer next to her bed. "The first few nights can be rough, so feel free to call the night nurse if you need her."

Lawrence left, and DC locked the door. She took the foil off the plates and looked at the food, but had no appetite. She'd felt dizzy and nauseous ever since she arrived, and she could feel the beginnings of a nasty headache. *Lawrence was right, withdrawal is going to be a bitch.*

She put on her pajamas and crawled into bed with *Dark of the Moon*. She managed to read a couple of chapters, but her headache was quickly becoming a migraine and her heart was racing. She reached for the nurse's bell several times but never pressed it. Finally, at 3 a.m., she fell asleep, thinking about 'that fuckin' Flowers,' as Sanford had nicknamed his hero.

29

AFTER AN EARLY DINNER WITH OMAR and Beth Ann at Ike's in Minnetonka, John and TJ checked into the Holiday Inn in Chanhassen. As he unlocked his door, John said, "See you in the morning. We have to be at police headquarters at nine o'clock, so let's meet for breakfast at 7:30 and we can review the plan."

"Sounds good," TJ replied. "Thanks again for bringing me out here. I'm realizing how much I needed a change of scenery." He closed his door and took off his shoes, then pulled the bedspread off the bed, stowed it in the closet, and lay down on the blanket. He dialed Da Boss's number, who answered instantly.

"How's your vacation?" Da Boss asked.

"Well, as you know, I'm not very good at relaxing, so I've managed to inject myself into a situation that I think you'll find very intriguing."

Da Boss laughed. "I suspected as much. What's going on up there in Lake Wobegon?"

"Get a piece of paper and I'll explain the cast of characters while you take notes." He explained how his dad knew John, John's connection to Omar, how Omar met Jake and Beth Ann, and how Jake discovered his special ability and ended up in jail.

When he finished, Da Boss whistled. "Holy shit, TJ, if what you're saying is true, this is powerful stuff. Can you imagine the implications?"

"I certainly can, which is why I need to get Jake get out of jail pronto."

"Well, you've got my permission to do whatever it takes. Tread lightly on the locals, but if they get in the way, I'll be more than happy to sic the U.S. Marshals on them. Hell, I'd even send them to Guantanamo Bay for a vacation."

TJ laughed, knowing Da Boss wasn't kidding. He took his job very seriously and didn't suffer fools who stood in the way. "Thanks, Boss. Wish me luck, and I'll be in touch."

No sooner had he hung up than his phone rang again. "One more thing. Don't forget my case of Spotted Cow," Da Boss said, and hung up.

TJ rolled off the bed, stripped down to his boxers, and brushed his teeth. He put his gun underneath his pillow and turned off the light.

▲ ▼ ▲

The next morning, he woke up early, since he was on East Coast time, and did a quick workout in the fitness center. He showered and put on a pair of khakis, a pressed cotton shirt, and a sport coat. He met John in the breakfast room, and they availed themselves of the free hard-boiled eggs, cold cereal, bagels with peanut butter, and donuts.

On the way over to the Minnetonka police headquarters, John explained the agenda. "We're meeting with the D.A., the police chief, and Detectives Gino Sweeney and George Washburn. Jake and Seth Morton, his attorney, will be on standby in another room."

"And I've got Da Boss on standby in Washington."

"What do you mean? I thought you told him you were on vacation."

"I did, but after realizing the magnitude of Jake's powers, I came clean and gave him the full story. As I knew he would be, he was mighty intrigued, so if these folks don't see things our way, he'll back us up with a couple of U.S. Marshals and a Guantanamo Bay getaway."

"Would he really do that?"

"Oh, yes, he would—and more."

"Holy shit, TJ."

When the men entered the police building, an officer was waiting for them by the reception desk. "Good morning, gentlemen. I'm Officer Nelson. Follow me." She led them to a conference room, where three men were seated around a long table with a plate of bagels and a cardboard container of coffee.

One of the men put down his bagel and walked toward John and TJ, his hand outstretched. "Good morning, gentlemen. I'm Dillon Matthews, District Attorney, and these are homicide detectives Gino Sweeney and George

Washburn." Gino stood up and nudged George, who hastily got to his feet.

"I'm John Michaud, and this is my colleague, TJ Janick." The men shook hands. TJ sat down at the head of the table and John took the chair on his right. Another man marched into the room. John stood up and extended his hand. "Hello, Mason, it's good to see you."

"Nice to see you, John. How the heck is Bayfield County doing these days?"

"Excellent. Mason, I'd like you to meet TJ Janick, special agent and senior officer in the Homeland Security Department of Countering Weapons of Mass Destruction."

"Hello, TJ. I know your father," Mason said. "He's a damn fine attorney. Give him my regards."

"Thank you, I'll be sure to do that." TJ took his badge out of his coat pocket and set it on the table.

John looked around at everyone. "As you know, I'm John Michaud, Chief of the Bayfield Police Department, and I'm sure you're wondering why I brought Homeland Security to your doorstep. TJ, I'll let you explain."

"We understand you've arrested Jake Silver for murder," TJ said.

"Yes, we have," Dillon replied proudly. "We have a rock-solid case against him."

John stifled a laugh, and George glared at him.

"Well, I'm sure you all believe that to be true, but I'm afraid you're mistaken," TJ said. "From our perspective, Mr. Silver could not have murdered anyone. Not with a blowgun, as you claim, or a rifle, or even a bazooka, for that matter. So, as of this moment, Mr. Silver is now under the jurisdiction of Homeland Security. We appreciate your efforts, but Chief Michaud and I respectfully demand that you, how should I say it?" He looked at John.

"I believe the term is stand down," John said with a grin.

"Thank you, John. That's exactly the term I was looking for. Effective immediately, you must stand down."

"The hell, you say!" Mason bellowed. He stood up, his face and ears as red as a Christmas ball. "You can't come riding in here on your governmental high horse and demand we stand down. Goddamn it!"

Dillon, who looked like he wanted to curl up in a ball and return to his mother's womb, opened his mouth to speak. "Actually, Chief, he can. In fact, he could have every one of us arrested and put in solitary confinement in some jail cell in Timbuktu with no trial and no legal representation. Ever since 9/11, everything's changed."

30

THERE WAS A BRISK KNOCK ON her door, and DC woke up with a start. It was followed by a louder rap. She sat up in bed, wondering where the hell she was. "Time to rise and shine, Ms. Krueger," a young woman's voice said. "It's nearly 7:00, and breakfast is being served in the cafeteria."

DC took a deep breath and tried to swing her legs over the bed, but nausea got the better of her, and she bent over and threw up all over the floor. The door opened, and the young woman hurried in with a key in her hand and a look of concern. "Oh, my, Ms. Krueger, let me help you."

DC fell back on her bed, curled up into a fetal position, shut her eyes, and let out a devil's moan. The young woman pushed a button to summon help and carefully stepped around the vomit. She sat down on the edge of DC's bed and put her a gentle hand on her shoulder. "Ms. Krueger, you'll be okay," she said in a soft voice. She began to stroke DC's back, repeating, "You will be okay. You will be okay," until DC went back to sleep.

▲ ▼ ▲

John drove back to Victoria with TJ riding shotgun. Jake, who was stretched out in the back seat, had the broadest grin on his face since he was eight years old and Santa Claus had delivered a ten-speed on Christmas morning. TJ had outlined his proposal, which Jake had all but accepted, pending approval from Beth Ann and Omar. He couldn't wait to get home, shower and shave, and sit outside on his deck. John parked the car in front of the garage. *Alleluia, I'm home!*

TJ got out and opened Jake's door. "Welcome home, Mr. Silver," he said with a smile. The front door swung open and Beth Ann ran down the path and jumped into Jake's arms. "Oh, sweetie, I've missed you so much!" She gave him a kiss worth remembering.

"Hey, Chief. Hey, TJ. Nice to see you again. Thanks for getting this guy out of jail," Omar said, slapping Jake on the back. "Jake, I know it's your house, but today, you're the guest of honor. Go on out to the deck with John and TJ, and Beth Ann and I will serve you."

Everyone helped themselves to Diet Cokes and Spotted Cows as John and TJ recounted the meeting at the Minnetonka police station. "So, Beth Ann and Omar, not only is Jake a free man, but you two are also covered by Homeland Security, so you can't be charged with murder, or anything else, for that matter," TJ said.

"Oh, wow!" Beth Ann said. "I was seriously worried, so this is a huge relief."

"Thanks, you guys!" Omar said. "This is great news."

"So what happens now?" Beth Ann asked.

"Jake, can I share the plan with them?" TJ said.

"Absolutely! They're my people."

"Well, I'm pleased to report that, pending your approval, Jake is going to accompany me to Washington, D.C., to meet Da Boss. Assuming the meeting goes well, Jake will be examined by several of the best doctors in the world. I anticipate they will take MRIs of his brain, conduct a series of examinations, and test his abilities. If everything checks out, he'll spend a couple of months getting into excellent physical shape as we establish usage guidelines."

"What do you mean, usage guidelines?" Beth Ann asked.

"Well, if Jake has this power, which I believe he does, Homeland Security will be first in line, closely followed by the FBI, the DEA, and other branches."

"Are you shitting me?" Omar asked.

"Omar, as I swear on this Spotted Cow, everything I'm saying is true. If my plan comes to fruition, and I have every confidence that it will, Jake is about to become America's newest hero."

31

AFTER THE WORST WEEK OF DC's life, her withdrawal symptoms began to ease. She'd finally regained her appetite, her nausea was mostly gone, and her dizziness was tolerable. She still wasn't sleeping through the night, but that gave her plenty of time to read. She'd finished three Virgil Flowers novels and was in the middle of the fourth, *Bad Blood.* She was madly in love with that fuckin' Flowers.

Just as Marlene had anticipated, she was finding solace in the group sessions. Serendipitously, she'd reconnected with a woman who'd gone to her high school. Her name was Trish Campbell. and she was two years older than DC. Back in high school, Trish was everything DC aspired to be. She had long, glossy raven hair, a movie-star face, and a perfect nose. She had dated Trevor "Biff" Johnson, the handsome quarterback, and in the fall of their senior year, they were named homecoming king and queen.

DC always thought Trish had the perfect life, which it was—until homecoming weekend. As DC learned in one of the group sessions, Trish had never touched drugs or alcohol until Biff made her drink a big cup of wapatoolie before the dance. She took the first sip just to make Biff happy, but then she discovered she liked the taste, since it reminded her of Hawaiian Punch. Biff neglected to tell her it was mixed with 190-proof Everclear, so she downed the first cup, and then a second. The day after the dance, she was shocked to learn she'd been the life of the party. She had no recollection of getting up on stage and dancing like Stevie Nicks while singing a very good cover of "Landslide," her favorite song.

Three months later, Trish threw up after breakfast, and her mother, recognizing the signs, took her to the pediatrician. When the doctor confirmed that Trish was pregnant, all hell broke loose. Her parents called a meeting with Biff and his parents, and everyone except Trish agreed she should have an abortion. She asked Biff to marry her, but he scoffed and broke up with her on the spot. He'd been offered a full scholarship to play football at the University of Arkansas, and nothing was going to stop him from achieving his dreams.

As Trish told DC, she'd had the abortion at a local hospital but never had any counseling, and she fell into a deep, dark depression. Racked with guilt and shame, she'd lie awake all night, tossing and turning. Late one night, she slipped downstairs, opened her parents' liquor cabinet, and made herself a drink. One drink became two, and, before long, she was drinking every night, and eventually, every day.

After graduation, she went to the University of Minnesota and joined a sorority. She fell into a routine of late-night drinks on weekdays and keg parties on weekends. Fortunately, the sorority mother, a wonderful woman named Jeanne Hudson, stepped in and got in her into rehab. Trish had been there for two months, so she was a huge help to DC and even encouraged her to start painting and drawing with her.

Lawrence was a wonderful source of support for both Trish and DC. As they learned, he'd also been an addict in high school, with whiskey as his go-to friend. As part of his recovery, he'd accepted Jesus Christ and become a born-again Christian. He offered each of them a Bible and invited them to join his weekly Bible study group. Trish declined, but DC accepted, and not just because she had a huge crush on him.

32

DA BOSS WAS TALKING TO someone on his desk phone, so Jake looked around his office. His gaze landed on a wall covered with photos. Many of them were obviously taken decades ago, since Da Boss looked so young. A couple of the photos jumped out at Jake. One was of a group of people in wet suits standing in the sand. Jake surmised they were Navy Seals, since the honorable Jesse Ventura, former governor of Minnesota and the only Navy Seal Jake had ever met, was in the picture. The other photo was of Da Boss and the president of the United States in the Oval Office. Da Boss was frowning, but the president had a big grin on his face and one arm draped over Da Boss's shoulder.

Da Boss pressed a button and ended the call. He stared across his enormous, polished wooden desk at Jake. "Welcome to Washington, D.C., Mr. Silver. I trust you had a good flight."

"Yes, thank you, sir. It was a great flight. I always enjoy the meals in first class."

"Well, given your special talent, we wouldn't want to put you in coach, where you might decide to start offing the flight attendants because you weren't happy with the food."

"Yes, that would be unfortunate."

"So here we are," Da Boss said, clasping his hands on his desk. "Mr. Silver, I must preface our conversation by saying that I sincerely hope this isn't some sort of Iranian, or, God forbid, Saudi Arabian charade. I'm not sure what the motive would be, other than finding amusement at the expense of the infidel Americans, but with more money than God, the Saudis could easily pull off a prank of this magnitude."

Jake nodded, unsure how to reply.

"Having said that, I hope you are the real deal, exactly as TJ has described. While I have come to rely on his usually impeccable judgment, I do need to verify your abilities through a number of channels. If it's confirmed that you do indeed have this power, you will make my year, not to mention my career."

▲ ▼ ▲

"I have never, ever, seen anything like this before." The speaker was Dr. Gretchen Sibyl, head neurologist at Georgetown University. Looking intently at Da Boss and TJ, she picked up her laser pointer and directed it at Jake's MRI. "Do you see these three small black circles and the gray striped area between them?" She drew a line between each circle to create a perfect triangle. "This is simply amazing," she said, tapping each circle with her laser. "These circles represent portions of the brain that are gone. They will never regain their function. But take a closer look at the gray area. Notice the stripes are wavy, yet equally spaced, and they don't connect at any point. The implications of this are extraordinary."

"As we expected," Da Boss said. "So then, what are the next steps?"

"I want to meet with Jake Silver as soon as possible," Dr. Sibyl said eagerly. "I'll also order a battery of tests so I can document the results and publish my findings in the Journal of the American Medical Association."

Da Boss stood up, removed the MRI from the frame, and handed it to TJ. "I'm sorry, Doctor, this is not going to be possible. In fact, you will not talk about Jake Silver and his MRI to anyone, ever. This is an issue of national security." He opened his jacket and pulled out his Homeland Security badge. "After all, you wouldn't want to spend the rest of your life in a prison cell, now would you?"

The startled neurologist shook her head.

"No, I didn't think you would."

The next six weeks were a whirlwind of activity. Jake was assigned to not one but two personal trainers. Both were Marines, but that's where the similarities stopped. One was an attractive woman with a Southern drawl, whom Jake nicknamed Dixie. Her counterpart was a short, muscular guy with a South Boston accent, so Jake called him Southie.

Every morning, Jake rose at 5:30 and went for a long run with Dixie and Southie. Every day, they added a mile or two, so he ended up running more than 20 miles, often finishing ahead of them. Even though he was short in stature, Southie pushed Jake relentlessly in the weight room. When Jake hit 200 pounds on the free weight bench, Southie nearly broke a smile.

Southie also spent hours with Jake on the gun range, reacquainting him with a rifle and teaching him how to use a handgun. On alternate days, Southie taught him how to fight with a knife. Dixie had her own set of skills, and she taught Jake how to pick most common locks in less than a minute. Even though he had no idea why he was learning to pick locks, he got a kick out of it.

Afternoons were reserved for dry runs supervised by TJ, since Da Boss wanted to keep Jake's powers hidden from as many people as possible for as long as possible. After lunch, TJ would drive Jake out to a vast open field in Virginia, where he'd watch him use his powers to kill mice, rabbits, raccoons, gophers, and even a small deer.

Every day, TJ would move Jake farther and farther away from the target and take notes while Jake used different combinations of finger pointing and finger wiggling with whispering, speaking, or loudly yelling "Just die."

By the end of the six weeks, Jake was in the best shape he'd been in since he was a high school athlete. He was fit and trim, with five new pounds of muscle. He had also developed a clear understanding of his powers. He and TJ had discovered that if the target was within 15 to 20 feet, he could simply point his finger and whisper, "Just die," and the target would die instantly. If the target was within 100 feet or even around a corner, he could wiggle his finger instead of pointing it and speak normally. But for targets that were 200–590 feet away, he had to point his finger and yell, "Just die" as loudly as he could.

▲ ▼ ▲

On the first day of week seven, Jake woke up to sun streaming through his window. He looked at the clock and smiled. It was nearly 9:00, so apparently there'd been no 5:30 run. He heard a knock on the door. "Who is it?"

"It's TJ. Get your ass out of bed. Da Boss wants to see us in 20 minutes."

"Yeah, what's he going to do if I'm late? Shoot me?"

"Probably."

Jake jumped out of bed, took a fast shower, and jogged to the lobby where TJ was waiting impatiently. He turned on his heel and led the way toward the mess hall, where Da Boss was sitting at a table.

Da Boss pointed at the buffet line. "Jake, I had them keep the buffet open for you. After all the hard work you've put in, I figure you deserve to sleep late. By the way, I had them prepare your favorite—eggs Benedict with melted cheddar cheese."

After Jake and TJ had finished eating, TJ topped up Jake's mug with more coffee. "Jake, we all appreciate how you have taken to our schedule," he said. "You've worked hard and never once complained. And believe me, your commitment has not gone unnoticed."

"Well, thanks, TJ. At first, I really didn't understand why I needed to get in shape and learn to shoot a handgun or rifle. Then it dawned on me that sometimes just saying "Just die" won't cut it, so I need to be able to cut and run or stand and defend myself."

"That's exactly right. By the way, this was an abbreviated training used by both the FBI and the CIA. I've been through it, and it's definitely come in handy, although I've never had to use my lock-picking skills."

Da Boss cleared his throat. "Jake, we'd originally planned to train you for three months. But we have an opportunity to use your skills immediately, which is what we want to talk to you about. The president of the Republic of Congo is speaking at the United Nations at the end of next week. He's been on our radar for quite some time, given that he's soliciting nuclear weapons. He's ruled his country since 1979, keeping his constituents happy with continued oil revenues. The Republic of Congo is the fourth-largest oil producer in the Gulf of Guinea, and the president feels that if he acquires nuclear weapons, he can unify Africa and rule the continent as a dictator. And I'm afraid he's right."

Jake put down his coffee mug and frowned. "I'm not sure I'm ready to kill someone at the United Nations, no matter how evil they are. I'd probably not make it past the guards, and if I did, I'm sure the place is filled with cameras."

Da Boss nodded. "Absolutely. That would be catastrophic for all of us. But fortunately, President Abrafo will be in northern California over the weekend. He's paying a visit to the Donner Memorial State Museum in Truckee."

"What's that about?" Jake asked.

"According to our sources, President Abrafo is fascinated with cannibalism, so he wants to visit the site of America's most famous cannibalistic event. It must run in the family, since his grandfather is rumored to have been a cannibal. Apparently, he had a fondness for eyeballs as an appetizer and deep-fried brains as an entree."

"And, because he wants to keep his visit under the radar, it's not appearing anywhere on his schedule," Da Boss said.

"So, there'll be no entourage, no cameras, and no press presence at the museum?" Jake asked.

"You got it," Da Boss replied with a smile.

33

IT WAS JAKE'S FIRST DAY ON the job at the Visitor Center at the Donner Memorial State Museum. He was sitting at the receptionist desk in the lobby of the rustic wooden building, looking dapper in a California State Parks uniform. At TJ's insistence, he'd dyed his hair black and grown a mustache. It was just past noon on Wednesday. The Visitor Center was empty, which wasn't unusual, since most visitors came up to Truckee on weekends. Which was why the president of the Republic of the Congo had picked that time to pay a visit.

Jake was subbing for the receptionist, who was on his lunch hour. As TJ's operatives had figured out, the guy was a creature of habit, so he always ate lunch at the Squeeze Inn Café, a seven-minute drive from the museum. At any moment, the guy was going to get pulled over for expired tabs or some other inane reason, so he wouldn't be back for at least an hour.

Shortly before noon, Jake greeted a solo guest, who bought five tickets and took a fast spin around the Visitor Center before leaving. Jake guessed he was the president's right-hand guy, but given the scowl on his face, he probably didn't share his boss's interest in cannibalism. At 12:15, the guy reappeared in the lobby and held the door open for an enormous black man, who was accompanied by three shorter men. Jake recognized the group from the images TJ had shared with him in Washington. The men were all dressed alike in dark suits with white shirts and polished black shoes.

The group began walking slowly around the Visitor Center. Jake watched as they paused at a display that acknowledged that members of the ill-fated Donner Party had eaten some of their companions. He choked down a tuna sandwich and tried to calm his shaking nerves.

He'd awoken in his hotel room after a fitful night's sleep, anticipating the day's agenda. He had just about canceled the entire operation and possibly his commitment to Homeland Security when his phone buzzed. It was a text from TJ. *Thanks again for your commitment to our country.* Jake looked at the text and sighed. He shook his head, got out of bed, took a hot shower, and put on his uniform.

By the time he'd finished his sandwich, the group had finished their tour and was headed for the entrance. One of the men held the door as the others filed out of the building, with the president bringing up the rear. Jake took a deep breath, pointed a shaking finger at the man's back, and whispered the deadly words under his breath.

Like a giant redwood struck by lightning, the president collapsed, smacking his head on a display case and cracking the glass. Blood spurted from a giant gash in his forehead. The guy at the door called to his colleagues, and they ran back into the building. They were bent over their boss, so they didn't notice Jake as he left the receptionist desk and made his way to the back door.

A black Chevy Suburban was idling outside. Jake opened the passenger door and threw himself onto the seat. TJ waited while he buckled his seat belt and then drove away from the Visitor Center.

"You okay?" TJ handed Jake a towel from the hotel. Jake looked at TJ and started to speak, but no words came out. He grabbed the towel and held it to his mouth. He threw up, the rank smell of half-digested tuna sandwich filling the car. TJ rolled down the windows and turned onto the main road. "Let it go, buddy. Just let it all go," he said quietly.

When they got to the hotel, Jake bolted from the SUV. TJ followed him as he sprinted blindly through the lobby, ignoring quizzical looks from a group of the hikers who were checking in. TJ helped him open his door, then drew the curtains and turned on the shower. "Rinse off, and then try to get some sleep," TJ said. "I'll be right next door, and I'll check on you in an hour."

Jake stripped off his uniform and stood under the hot water for ten minutes. He used the entire bottle of shampoo and then washed his hair again, trying to erase the memory of the dead president, his face covered with blood and his blank eyes staring at the ceiling, frozen like a member of the Donner Party. Jake got out of the shower, dried off, and got under the covers. He lay there, shaking and shuddering, until he finally fell asleep.

▲ ▼ ▲

The phone on the bedside table rang, startling Jake awake. "It's TJ. You've been sleeping for twelve hours. Are you okay?"

"Are you freaking kidding me? I just killed a man, so no, I'm not okay."

"I get it," TJ said quietly.

"I sure hope you get it. This wasn't just a goddamn hog farmer who murdered two deputies with wives and young kids. This was the president of a freaking country. So as you might have guessed, I'm feeling guilty as shit, and I'm done with this just die garbage, and I quit." Jake slammed the phone into the cradle and picked it up again. He pressed the button for the front desk.

"Front desk. How may I help you?"

"Hi, this is Jake Silver in Room 304."

"Yes, Mr. Silver. How may I be of service today?"

"There's a suspicious guy following me, so don't put any calls through to my room. He's in his late thirties with short brown hair and an athletic build. If he knocks on my door, I want him escorted from the premises immediately."

"Oh, my, Mr. Silver. I'm so sorry. Would you like me to call the police?"

"Sure. Do whatever you think is necessary."

Ten minutes later, Jake heard voices in the hall. He got out of bed and put on a pair of shorts and a T-shirt. He looked through the peephole and stifled a laugh. TJ was standing in the hallway, being questioned by two local cops. One was a large red-headed man who could have been Paul Bunyan's cousin, while the younger cop, a slight man with a blond buzz cut, appeared to be fresh out of officer training. "Hands in the air, sir," the older cop said. TJ did as instructed, and the cop spotted his shoulder holster.

"Ah, I get it. You're armed. Hands on the wall and spread your legs. I'm sure you know the drill." Jake watched as TJ complied. The younger cop wrangled TJ's sport coat off his shoulders, and the older cop took his gun.

"While you're at it, go ahead and grab my wallet, officer," TJ said. "It's in my front right pocket."

The cop reached inside TJ's coat and removed the wallet. He flipped it open and whistled. "Son of a bitch." He showed the Homeland Security badge to his partner.

TJ held out a hand. The cop dropped the wallet into TJ's palm. TJ slipped it into his pants pocket and held his hand out again. "Now give me back my gun. As you both understand, it belongs to the Department of Homeland Security, and if you don't quit screwing around, I'll have both of you thrown in your own jail."

"Oh, for Chrissakes, let's not overreact. We're on the same side, after all."

"Now scram," TJ said. The officers scurried away down the hall.

TJ put his eye to the peephole. "Nice work, Mr. Silver. Now open this goddamn door."

Jake opened the door as far as the chain would allow and grinned at TJ.

"Glad you're amused. Da Boss wants to have a word with you, so quit playing around and put some clothes on."

"Da Boss is here in Truckee?" Jake's smile disappeared.

"Of course he is. You've got ten seconds to get dressed."

Jake shut the door, put on a pair of pants and a shirt, ran a brush through his hair, and gargled with the hotel mouthwash. He undid the chain and opened the door. TJ nodded and led the way to the hotel dining room.

Da Boss was sitting at a table in the corner, his back to the room. TJ and Jake sat down. He looked at his watch and then stared at Jake. "So, Jake. How'd it go?"

"Not so well."

"Yes, I can imagine."

"Can you? Can you really?" TJ put his hand on Jake's arm. Jake brushed it away and continued. "Can you actually imagine what it feels like to kill someone and watch them die in a puddle of their own blood?"

"Yes, as a matter of fact, I can," Da Boss replied quietly.

"I'm sorry, sir. Of course you can. It's just that I really hate blood. It always makes me upchuck."

"That's exactly what my dearly departed mother used to say," Da Boss said with a smile. "It's unfortunate that the president happened to fall on that glass case, and I'm sorry about your hemophobia. We'll take note of that with your next assignment."

"Hell, no!" Jake said.

"What did you say?"

"I think you both heard me." Jake looked at Da Boss and TJ. "There won't be a next assignment. I'm done with this crap. It's not a good use of my time. I want to go home, get married, raise half a dozen kids, and lead a normal life."

Da Boss nodded. "Now that would be nice. Hell, I've thought about that myself, off and on. But then 9/11 happened, and I gave up on that dream. But Jake, TJ and I are not asking you to give up your dream. We're only asking you to put your dream on hold."

"I don't think I can do that."

"Listen, Jake. I don't want to waste my time or yours," Da Boss said. "If you abandon Homeland Security, we will have no choice but to step away from supporting you and your fiancée. Both of you would likely be charged with homicide, so don't even go there. I'm not here to bully you, but I do believe you're God's gift to the American people. You have the power to tilt the scales in our favor, so I'm not going to let you step away from this responsibility. Never forget that the real power belongs to me and me alone. If I decide to point my finger at you and say, 'Just die,' you're dead."

Da Boss held up his finger and pointed it at Jake. A red laser beam in the shape of a sniper's cross instantly appeared on Jake's chest. Jake looked down at his shirt. His mouth dropped open, and his heart took off at a gallop.

"*Capiche*, Jake?" Da Boss put down his finger and the red mark disappeared as quickly as it had appeared. "Good. Now let's be friends and return to the topic at hand. Forget the broken glass, forget the blood, and let's focus on what you just accomplished for the good of America and the good of the world. That man you killed was going to use nuclear weapons to rule Africa. You've changed the course of history. Think about that."

Jake nodded.

"Jake, you're a hero, even if your fellow American citizens don't know it." Da Boss nodded at TJ, who unrolled a radiograph on the table.

"What is this?" Jake asked.

"It's your MRI, Jake." Da Boss took a Montblanc Meisterstück pen out of his pocket and traced the triangles. "It's one in a million, or, to be more accurate, one in a hundred billion. I believe that you've been given a gift, and as you know, every gift comes with a responsibility. Think of it as a form of patriotic *noblesse oblige*. To quote the apostle Luke, 'from everyone to whom much has been given, much will be required.'"

"You sound like my mother," Jake said with a wry grin.

"Thank you. Even though I am a man of science, I believe there are no coincidences. You're here on Earth for a reason, and you're at this table with TJ and me for a reason. As an American, you're lucky enough to be one of the good guys. If fate had dealt you a different hand, you'd be a citizen of a different country and, as soon as their government discovered your powers, guess what?"

"I'd be killing Americans."

"Damn straight. Along with the British, the French, the Israelis, and our other allies."

Jake looked at Da Boss and TJ and took a deep breath. "Okay. What's next?"

34

TWO HOURS LATER, JAKE FOUND himself in a Boeing C-40 Clipper, watching Lake Tahoe get smaller and smaller as the plane climbed through the clouds. He was sitting in a lounge chair, facing TJ and Da Boss. A flight attendant handed them each a crystal tumbler of single-malt scotch.

"Cheers, Jake. Nice work." TJ held up his glass. "Drink up, since we'll be landing in Colorado before you know it. Your target is Pablo Blanco, the largest drug lord in Mexico, but it should be relatively easy, since he's safely ensconced in Florence ADX, a.k.a. the Alcatraz of the Rockies."

"Wait a sec. If you've already captured him, why is he my next target?"

"Because he's already escaped twice. And next time—and there will be a next time, since he has more money than God—he's likely to kill the Mexican president, which may or may not be a good thing. But he's also sworn to kill our president, along with the first lady and their four kids, because that's what goddamn drug lords do. They think nothing of slaughtering entire families in their beds, just because they can."

Jake shook his head. "I still don't get it. Why do you need me? Can't you just off him in his cell?"

"No way, José, I mean Jake," Da Boss said with a grin. "He's in solitary confinement with no access to the general population, so if he got killed in his cell, his attorneys would sue us for all the gold in Fort Knox."

"But he's allowed to see his beloved wife once a month," TJ said. "So if you're a prison guard and you just happen to be on duty tomorrow, you can use your superpower, just like you did earlier today."

"Okay, I get the picture," Jake said. "He's talking to his wife and he suddenly collapses, either of a massive heart attack or an aneurysm."

"Exactly," Da Boss said. "And while the other guards spring to his aid, you slip out of the room, and the rest, as we might say, is American history."

▲ ▼ ▲

The next morning, TJ stopped at the first guard tower at ADX Florence. He presented his badge, and he and Jake waited as the guards scanned the Escalade before waving them through. "Welcome to living hell," TJ said. He pointed to the 12-foot razor fence surrounding the compound. He pulled up to the door and put the SUV in park. "You ready for this?"

Jake nodded. He opened his door, feeling the weight of his brand-new Walther PPQ handgun nestled in a leather holster under his arm. He gave TJ a thumbs-up.

"Good luck to you, Jake," TJ said as he pulled away from the curb.

Jake slung his duffel bag over his arm, reached in his jacket pocket, pulled out his Homeland Security badge, and flashed it at the guard.

"Homeland Security! Don't see many of you guys around here. Hey, how do I get a gig like that?" he whispered as he slipped a card into Jake's hand. Jake pocketed the card and kept walking through the lobby per TJ's instructions. When he reached the far wall, another guard was standing behind a thick layer of bulletproof glass. Jake pushed his badge through the small opening.

The guard nodded. "Special Agent Silver, the warden is expecting you. I'll show you to his office." He pressed a button, and Jake heard the click of a lock. A door swung open, and the guard motioned to Jake to follow him. He led him down a hall to a large office, where a slight man sat behind a desk. The man stood up and held out a soft, well-manicured hand.

"Good morning, Mr. Silver, I'm Warden Ward Armstrong."

Jake shook the man's hand and stifled a grin.

"The answer is yes, it's my real name," Ward replied.

"How'd you know what I was thinking?"

"Happens all the time. My name is Bradley Ward Armstrong, and I used to be a hair stylist in Pueblo, where I still live. It's not a bad commute—only about 45 minutes each way—and, as you can imagine, there's very little traffic. Back in Pueblo, I go by Brad. But I was getting tired of being on my feet all day, so when one of my customers told me about this job, I decided to switch up my life and become Warden Ward Armstrong."

"Makes sense to me." Jake made a mental note to tell Beth Ann and Omar about Ward the Warden.

▲ ▼ ▲

TJ was eating a plate of enchiladas at a roadside café when his phone buzzed with a text from Da Boss. *Talk to me.*

I dropped him off about an hour ago, TJ texted back. *As we agreed, I didn't give him a chance to renege. I'm eating lunch, and then I'll head back and get him.*

Let's hope there's no upchucking! Da Boss replied, adding a row of vomiting emojis.

▲ ▼ ▲

Jake buttoned up his shirt and looked at himself in the mirror of the dressing room. *Not bad for an ex-Wall Street guy.* He admired how his newly dark hair and mustache matched the black epaulets on his gray shirt. He stuffed his clothes and his gun into his duffel bag and put them in a locker. He went out to the hallway, and Ward led him to the visitor's room, where the regular guard was more than happy to take an extended smoke break.

Jake stood in the corner and surveyed the room, which held only a small table and two hard chairs. Another guard entered the room, escorting a voluptuous brunette dressed in black. He pointed to one of the chairs, and she sat down. The guard left the room. The woman gave Jake the once-over before looking down at the table. Ten minutes later, the door opened again and two guards led Pablo Blanco into the room. He was heavily shackled, and he stumbled over to the chair across from his wife. The guards ran a chain through a steel ring buried in the table and clipped it to another ring on the man's back. They took their positions on either side of the door and nodded at Jake.

To Jake's surprise, Blanco began to sing quietly to the woman. She smiled and sang back to him. Jake strained to hear the words and realized they were singing *"Da La Vuelta,"* a salsa song by Marc Anthony. *"Que te olvidaste de mi. Que se ha escapado el amor. Por el portal del astio,"* the drug lord crooned. Jake did his best to recall his high school Spanish and translated as he sang: "That you forgot about me. That love has escaped. Through the portal of boredom."

The wife smiled and sang, *"Da la vuelta y vete ya. Hoy te doy la libertad. De volar a donde quieras."* Blanco nodded. Jake caught his breath as he translated, "Leave already, leave already, leave already, wherever you want. I give you liberty."

Realizing that they were singing about an escape, Jake took a deep breath and pointed his finger at the drug lord while his wife was still singing. He whispered, "Just die," and then added *"Solo muere"* for good measure.

Blanco coughed, clutched his chest, and lurched sideways, hitting his head on the steel ring embedded in the table. He muttered, *"Oh mierda,"* and his eyes rolled back in his head.

The guards ran over to the table, and one pushed the wife back down into her chair. The other guard pulled the man up by his shoulders, but his body was limp. When the woman saw her husband's blank stare, she started wailing in Spanish. Jake slipped out the door and waited for the warden, who was hurrying down the hallway.

"What the hell just happened in there?" Ward said.

"Beats me. Blanco and his wife were singing some romantic Spanish love song to each other, and all of a sudden he slumped over and hit his head on the table. I'm thinking he must have had a heart attack. Maybe all the emotion of seeing his wife got to him."

▲ ▼ ▲

Jake went back to the dressing room and sent TJ a text. *Done.* He retrieved his duffel bag from the locker and headed for the exit. The guard in the lobby nodded at him and unlocked the door, allowing him to step out into the sunshine. Less than a minute later, TJ pulled up, and Jake climbed into the SUV. "You okay?" TJ asked.

"Yup. No blood and guts this time."

"Nice work. You can tell me more on the way home."

Fifteen minutes later, they arrived at the Fremont County Airport, where the plane was waiting for them. They settled into the lounge chairs, and the flight attendant poured the rest of the scotch into their glasses. Jake regaled TJ with the story, including his conversation with Warden Ward Armstrong. When he got to the part where Blanco and his wife sang a Spanish duet about leaving, TJ's eyes widened.

"Holy shit, Jake. I'm sure you're right. She was setting him up for an escape, and if you hadn't been there, he'd be on his way back to Mexico and his goons would be headed for Washington. I'm calling Da Boss now, and then he can circle back with the fine folks at Florence ADX." TJ dialed Da Boss's number and handed the phone to Jake.

"What the hell took you so long, TJ?" Da Boss said.

"It's not TJ. This is Jake on TJ's phone."

"Even better. What's the good word?"

"Solo muere."

Da Boss guffawed. "Music to my ears. Tell me everything."

Jake skipped the part about Ward and told him about the duet and how Blanco keeled over and hit his head. "Thankfully, there was no blood," he added.

"Jake Silver, I've said it before, but it bears repeating. You are a true American hero. I sincerely hope that one day your fellow citizens will understand the magnitude of your contributions to our country."

"Thank you, sir. Now, if it's all right with you, I'd like to take some time off."

"Didn't TJ tell you? The pilot is stopping in Minneapolis so you can get a jump start on your holidays. Now hand the phone to TJ, and I'll see you in the new year."

"Very good, sir." Jake passed the phone to TJ. The flight attendant appeared with a new bottle of scotch and topped up his glass. He took a long sip, leaned back in his seat, and closed his eyes.

35

JAKE WOKE UP IN HIS OWN BED on Saturday morning. He swung his legs over the edge and put on his slippers. Beth Ann opened her eyes and smiled at him. "I'm so glad they gave you a month off," she said.

"Me too. I guess that's one of the perks of being a special agent. Speaking of perks, want a cup of coffee?"

"No thanks, honey. I'm going to sleep a bit more. But later, after breakfast, we should look at the calendar. Omar wants to get together before he goes up to Bayfield for Christmas. Oh, and one more thing. We're meeting my mom tomorrow at Ike's."

Jake cringed. "Your dad won't be there, will he?"

Beth Ann sighed. "Yes, unfortunately. But he's not getting any younger, and I haven't seen him in a couple of years, so I said we could do brunch. I hope that's okay."

"Well, you and I both know it's not okay, given what your father did to you. But if it will make your mom happy, I'm willing to play along. You and I also know there's a special place in hell for ministers who abuse their daughters, so his time will come."

"Amen to that. Thank you for understanding, honey."

"Anything for you, sweetheart." He kissed her. "After all, you saved my life, so I owe you. Now, sweet dreams, and I'll make breakfast when you wake up."

Jake made coffee and unloaded the dishwasher. He ate a banana and looked out the window. A couple of guys on electric bikes were powering through the new snow on the trail. He sat down at the kitchen table and turned on his laptop. He sipped his coffee and reviewed his email messages. The first was from a woman named Natasha Rubling, informing him that someone had left him a million dollars. All he needed to do was confirm his address and his Social Security number and provide his bank account number, and the money would be transferred instantly. He googled the Croatian words for just die, pointed his finger at the email message, and whispered, *"Samo Umri."* When nothing happened, he grinned, forwarded the message to TJ, and deleted it.

▲ ▼ ▲

The next day, Jake and Beth Ann went to Ike's and snagged the large, horseshoe-shaped booth by the bar. Billy, Jake's favorite bartender, was squeezing fresh oranges into a glass pitcher. "Well, if it isn't Jake and Beth Ann!" Billy said. "Welcome back! How about a couple of mimosas?"

"Thanks, but no thanks, Billy. I'm in training, so make mine an Arnie Palmer, please, and a Cosmo, chilled to the bone, for Beth Ann."

Billy set the drinks on the table. "Happy holidays to you, my friends. These are on the house." Moments later, the hostess led Beth Ann's parents to the booth. Beth Ann stood up and gave her mother a hug, but pointedly ignored her father. Jake extended his hand to Frank, who responded with a limp handshake.

"Still drinking the hard stuff, Beth? Don't you know it'll kill you?" Frank said.

Beth Ann picked up her glass and held it in the air. "Fuck you, Dad, and the horse you rode in on." Beth Ann's mother gasped but didn't say a word.

"I guess I deserve that," Frank said with a snicker.

"You sure do, and a whole lot more." Beth Ann drained her glass and waved to the bartender. "One more, Billy, please. And this time, make it stronger."

"Hey, Beth Ann and Jake, welcome back!" the server said, as he set four menus on the table.

"Hi, Aaron, it's nice to be back! Aaron, this is my mom Marilyn and her husband Frank."

"Nice to meet you folks," Aaron said. "Hey, listen, Jake, I was super sorry to hear about your stroke. But I've gotta say, you look great. Have you been working out?"

"Sure have," Jake said with a grin.

Frank cleared his throat. "Excuse me, waiter, bus boy, whatever you are. I hate to break up this old home week, but my wife and I would each like a glass of sherry. That is, if it's not too much trouble for you."

"Certainly, sir. Two glasses of sherry, coming right up."

The four of them made small talk until the food arrived. Frank ordered another glass of sherry, and then another, so by the time they were finished eating, his face was flushed and the veins on his bulging nose were bright red.

When Aaron set the bill in the middle of the table, Jake waited to see if Frank would take it, since his wife had arranged the meeting. But instead, he pushed the bill at Jake. "Thanks for the meal, Jake," Frank said, without a trace of gratitude in his voice. "You're obviously a regular here, so I'm guessing they give you a substantial discount."

He looked at Beth Ann. "Now, before we leave, I want to say a few words. Beth Ann, I know you're still angry with me for the things that happened while you were growing up. But as I know you understand, I had my demons, namely, hard alcohol. So, at this point in our lives, it's time to forgive and forget, especially since I'll be marrying you in my church."

Beth Ann fell back against the booth, gasping for breath. Jake put his arms around her and held her tight. Beth's mother stood up, the blood draining from her face, and headed for the ladies' room.

"Goddamn it, are you freaking kidding me?" Beth Ann hissed. "For Chrissakes, you raped me damn near every day for I don't know how many years, and now you have the gall to suggest that I forgive and forget? I've always known you were a pedophile and a sex addict, but if you're thinking you're marrying Jake and me in your church, you're also a delusional sociopath."

Frank folded his hands and smiled benevolently. "No, Beth Ann. I'm a minister, and my congregation is expecting me to officiate at your wedding, so that's exactly what will happen."

"No freaking way. What the hell made you think I'd ever agree to that? Oh, wait, were you planning to kidnap Jake and me in the parking lot and throw us in the back of your stupid-ass Buick and drive us to your hypocritical church for a fake wedding?"

"Why would I need to do that? I've got this." He reached behind his back, pulled out a revolver, and waved it in her face. "If you and Jake don't agree right now to let me marry you in my church, I'll shoot both of you right here and then kill myself. Imagine your mother's face when she comes back from the ladies' room and we're all dead." He started to laugh hysterically.

Beth Ann stared at him and clutched Jake's hand. "My God, you're serious! You are fucking out of your mind, aren't you?"

"I sure am," Frank said, his face lighting up with demonic delight. "Didn't your mother ever tell you I'm proudly bipolar and borderline? And you, my little tart, were only one of my many dalliances. But you were always my favorite because you loved me, and you always did what I said and never told anyone, not even your sainted mother, even though she knew exactly what I was doing."

Beth Ann's eyes filled with tears. "Jake, please. Please say it. Say the words."

"Say what words?" Frank asked. His finger tightened on the trigger.

Jake inhaled, pointed his finger at Frank, and whispered, "Just die, you son of a bitch."

Frank dropped his gun and fell sideways out of the booth. His body landed on the floor at the exact moment Marilyn returned from the ladies' room. She looked at the gun on the table and then at Beth Ann and Jake and started to sob.

36

THE FOLLOWING SATURDAY, THE doorbell rang at 10 a.m. on the dot. "Omar's here!" Beth Ann called out. Omar was standing on the doorstep with gifts in his hands.

"Merry Christmas, Beth Ann!" Omar took off his coat and wrapped her up in a big hug. "Where's Jake?"

"He's in the kitchen, making eggs Benedict for us."

Jake was at the stove, stirring a pot of sauce.

"Oh, man, real hollandaise! My favorite!" Omar stuck his finger into the pan.

"Step away from my stove or I'll point my finger at you!" Jake slapped Omar's hand with the whisk. "Now both of you sit down while I put the finishing touches on your breakfast." Beth Ann filled their cups with coffee.

There were two gifts on Omar's placemat, and he shook the largest one. "They say the best gifts come in small packages, but I think it's the opposite. I'm all about large gifts. What the hell is in here?"

"Go ahead and open it!" Beth Ann said. "You're going to love it."

Omar untied the bow and tore the wrapping off the heavy box. He lifted the lid and whistled. "Holy shit, you guys. This is next level." He pulled out a leather shoulder holster with his initials embossed on the side. "Wow. This is way better than stuffing my SIG behind my back."

"Nothing but the best for you, my friend," Jake said.

"Open your other gift!" Beth Ann said.

Omar opened the box and held up a silver frame with an autographed photo of Vince Lombardi. The frame was engraved with the words Run to Daylight.

"You guys are the best. For once, I'm speechless."

"Now let's eat," Jake said. "Eggs Benedict wait for no man or woman."

"Okay, but then you have to open my gifts," Omar said.

They made short work of breakfast, and Omar handed Jake a heavy box. He unwrapped the package, revealing a dark green leather box embossed with the Green Bay Packers logo. "Omar, is this what I think it is?" Jake asked.

"Maybe!"

Jake lifted out a glass case resting on a mahogany base. Inside the case was a Green Bay Packers Super Bowl football autographed by Omar and every player on the winning team. Jake grinned. "Omar Carter, you are something else."

"Merry Christmas, Silverado. I hope you like it."

"Like it? I love it! But Omar, I know exactly how much these things cost, and there's no way I can accept it."

"And there's no way I can return it, so you have to keep it. And besides, now that my circumstances have changed, I can easily afford it."

"What do you mean?" Beth Ann asked.

"Well, as you guys know, I've made a bunch of stupid mistakes in my life, but I've also made a couple of smart moves. Five years ago, I invested five million dollars in the Templeton Square private real estate fund. It was a five-year term with a ten percent dividend, and it just expired. Thanks to the uptick in the real estate industry, it's turned out to be an even better investment than I anticipated, so I can easily afford nice gifts for my two best friends. Now open yours, Beth Ann."

He handed her a small flat box. Inside was an envelope with the Minnesota Vikings logo. She pulled out four season tickets and clutched them to her chest.

"Oh, my God, Omar, I can't believe this. I've always dreamed of having Vikings season tickets, and I can't believe you just gave them to me."

"To be honest, I can't believe I'm going to be sitting at US Bank Stadium with you and watching the Minnesota Vikings, but hey, that's what friends are for. Now, how about another cup of coffee, and then I want to hear about everything that's happened since I last saw you guys."

Jake reached behind him and took his wallet off the counter. He flipped it open and flashed it at Omar. "Happy holidays from Homeland Security."

"Holy smoly, Jake! Is that real?"

"Sure is," Beth Ann said. "I can't wait for you to hear all about Jake's accomplishments, including the much-deserved death of my abusive sociopathic bipolar pedophile father last weekend."

"Wait, Beth Ann, what did you just say?" Omar asked.

"You heard me. My dad was an ordained minister and the devil, all in one person. Jake and I had brunch with him and my mom at Ike's last Sunday, and he informed me that he intended to marry us in his church. When I said no, he pulled out a pistol and threatened to kill Jake and me right there at the table before killing himself, so I asked Jake to say the words, and he did."

"So what happened?"

"Jake pointed his finger, and my dad just keeled over and died. He fell on the floor and landed at my mother's feet. Jake and the manager dragged his body outside, and then the manager called the police and told them it wasn't an emergency. I ordered another glass of sherry for my mom and a round of drinks for everyone in the restaurant. When the bartender handed the sherry to my mom, she took a sip and declared, 'God works in mysterious ways!' By the time the Minnetonka police finally showed up, she was smiling from ear to ear."

"Yikes. That's heavy stuff. I'm really sorry. Good thing I wasn't there, otherwise I would have killed him myself."

"Thanks, Omar," Jake said. "I never intended to use my power on him, but when he threatened us, all my Homeland Security training kicked in, and I knew I had to protect Beth Ann and rid the world of another evil person."

"Yes, thank you, Omar, but no need to be sorry," Beth Ann said. "My dad was a sick, deranged monster, and, now that he's dead, I feel a huge sense of relief. All my anger is gone, and I don't even feel like swearing anymore. I almost feel like I've been born again. Now I can focus on taking care of Jake and becoming a veterinarian."

"Good for you, Beth Ann," Omar said. "May all your dreams come true—and may your dad rest in the hell he so richly deserves."

"Hear, hear!" Jake got up to make another pot of coffee.

▲ ▼ ▲

A week later, Jake and Beth Ann drove out to the small town where she grew up. They pulled into the church parking lot, which was nearly empty. They were just about to go inside when Beth Ann heard her mother's voice. "Yoohoo, Beth Ann and Jake! Wait up!"

Marilyn and a well-built younger man in a dark suit were walking toward them. Beth Ann did a double take. This woman bore no resemblance to the somber, brow-beaten woman they'd seen at Ike's. Her mother's newly blonde hair glinted in the sunlight, and she was wearing high-heeled black boots and a faux fur coat over a bright red pantsuit that matched her lipstick.

"Hi, honey. Hi, Jake," she called out. "I'd like you to meet my trainer, Tyler Duffy."

"Hi, Beth Ann. Hi, Jake," Tyler said. "I'd like to say I'm sorry about your loss, but based on everything Marilyn's told me, it sounds like congratulations are in order."

Beth Ann started to laugh. "Mother, what on earth is going on? I've never seen you like this."

"That's because I've never been like this before!" Marilyn replied with a mischievous smile. She lowered her voice to a whisper. "Beth Ann, I hated your father as much as you did, but I was deathly afraid of him. He told me if I ever left him, he'd hunt me down and shoot me, and then kill you and Jake while you slept. Every night, I'd pray for divine intervention, but I never dreamed that God would strike him down like that. It was the answer to all my prayers!"

"And to mine," Beth Ann said. "Now don't you think we should go inside?"

"Yes, I suppose. But first, let me tell you a few things. Now don't be surprised when you don't see an expensive coffin. I had your dad cremated, so his ashes are in a cheap-ass cardboard box on the altar."

"Oh, my gosh, Mom, that's ballsy of you. Dad always said he'd hate to be cremated."

"Almost as much as he hated my cat Blackberry." Marilyn giggled. "After the service, I'm bringing his ashes home and sprinkling them in Blackberry's litter box so she can shit and pee all over him."

"Mom!" Beth Ann burst out laughing. and Jake and Tyler joined in. "This is wonderful. I'm so proud of you."

"And two more things." Marilyn opened her Gucci purse and pulled out a baggie with a white-wrapped bundle inside. "This is your dad's gun. When he fell on the floor, I put it in one of Ike's napkins and took it home. Jake, I want you to sell it for scrap metal or whatever the hell else you want to do with it."

"My pleasure!" Jake said.

"What's the second thing?" Beth Ann asked.

"Thanks to the generosity of the ministry, your dad had a life insurance policy." Marilyn smiled and took an envelope out of her purse. "Since I was so blessed to be his wife, I was his sole beneficiary, and I just received this check for one million dollars. Whenever you and Jake decide to get married, I'll pay for your wedding and your honeymoon. Just promise me you won't get married in this church."

"Promise!" Beth Ann and Jake replied in unison. Beth Ann linked arms with her mother, and they skipped up the path to the entrance. Jake and Tyler held the double doors open for the women and followed them into the sanctuary, where the organist was playing "How Great Thou Art."

37

ON CHRISTMAS MORNING, JAKE and Beth Ann were at Jake's father's house in Stevens Point, Wisconsin. Beth Ann was showing off a Tiffany pearl necklace that Jake had given her the night before. They were just about to open more gifts when Jake's cell phone chirped. It was TJ, so he answered immediately. "Greetings, TJ!"

"And to you, Jake. Listen, I'm really sorry to interrupt your festivities, but I wanted to give you a heads-up. You're about to get an important phone call."

Jake got up from the sofa and walked into the kitchen. "And what exactly do you mean by important?"

"I mean important as in presidential. You're about to get a call from the Commander in Chief."

"Yikes. As in the president of the United States?"

"The one and only." TJ hung up, and Jake's phone rang again with a call from an unknown number.

"Hi, this is Jake Silver."

"Good morning, Mr. Silver," a woman said. "Please hold for the president."

"Certainly." Jake walked back into the living room where Beth Ann and his father were unwrapping gifts. As he sat down on the edge of the sofa, he made a shushing motion with his finger, and they all fell silent.

"Merry Christmas, Mr. Silver," the president said.

"Thank you, Mr. President. Merry Christmas to you." Jake's father and Beth Ann grinned at him in disbelief.

"Jake, my apologies for calling on a holiday, but I've got an issue. And after hearing about your recent successes in California and Colorado, I suspect you'll be able to help solve it."

"Thank you, Mr. President. To be honest, I had no idea you knew anything about me or what I've been doing."

"Word travels fast in these circles," the president said with a laugh. "Your talents are impressive, and I'm excited to have you on our team."

"Flattery will get you everywhere, Mr. President. I'm honored to help."

"And I'm equally honored that you're willing to use your talents in service to our country. Now, as you can imagine, I can't say any more over the phone. Hell, the Chinese are probably listening to our conversation. But I look forward to discussing this issue with you in person. How's Tuesday?"

"Um, yes, certainly. Tuesday will be fine. Thank you, Mr. President."

"Thank you, Jake. Have a Merry Christmas, and I'll see you next week."

The president hung up, and Jake burst out laughing. "Holy shit, you guys, that was the Commander in Chief!"

"Nice work, Jake," his dad said, tossing him a package. "Let's finish unwrapping all these gifts, and then you can explain why POTUS is calling you on Christmas morning."

▲ ▼ ▲

Jake's plane landed at Landmark Aviation at Dulles on Monday night at 9 p.m. The driver pulled up in front of the Watergate Hotel, got out of the limo, and spoke to the bellman. The bellman nodded and took Jake directly up to his suite. On the credenza was a silver tray with a bottle of The Macallan 25-year-old Scotch, a crystal tumbler, and a heavy white envelope. Jake opened the envelope and pulled out a handwritten note that read *Thanks again for your help* followed by a scribbled signature.

The bellman put Jake's suitcase in the closet and left the room. Jake poured himself a glass of scotch and stared down at the Potomac River, wondering what the president wanted him to do.

The next morning, Jake woke up early, ordered a pot of coffee and a plate of eggs and bacon from room service, and got dressed. The temperature was 45 degrees, mild by Minnesota standards, so he put on the new white Eaton shirt that Beth Ann had given him for Christmas, dark gray wool pants, a vintage camel cashmere sport coat that he'd borrowed from his dad, and his favorite Jerry Garcia tie. He checked his watch. It was 8 a.m., and the White House was a twenty-minute walk from the hotel, so he quickly flossed his teeth, gargled with the hotel mouthwash, went down to the lobby, and exited onto Virginia Avenue.

He turned left on New Hampshire, took a slight right on H Street, and a right onto Pennsylvania Avenue. When he reached the White House, he stopped and pulled out his phone. The last time he'd been here was in high school, when his history teacher had taken his class on a field trip during spring break. He held up his phone and took a selfie with the magnificent building in the background and texted it to his dad, Beth Ann, and Omar. Per TJ's instructions, he walked up to the visitors' entrance, took out his wallet, and handed his Homeland Security badge to the guard. Jake watched as the guard examined his badge and typed his name into a computer.

"Yes, good morning, Mr. Silver," the guard said, handing back the badge. "The president is expecting you. Please wait here, and a guard will escort you to the Oval Office."

▲ ▼ ▲

"Goddamn it, sir, you can't just waltz this killer into your office like he's a celebrity," snapped Emmitt Butcher, the president's chief of staff. "Mr. President, let's assume that what you're saying is true—which, by the way, I don't believe for a moment. This hayseed from Nowheresville, U.S.A. could point his finger at you, whisper his magic words, and poof, the president of the free world is history."

"Would you do me a favor and calm the fuck down? I appreciate your concern, but according to several people who I—and you—trust, this guy's the real deal. Based on everything I've heard, I think he's the miracle worker I need to break the impasse with Kim Jong-un."

"Well, that actually could be useful."

"Exactly. Look, I need to kick this new year off with a bang. My numbers are slipping, and if we can't turn them around *tout de suite*, I could very well lose the next election, which means you and I will be promptly put out to pasture."

"Unfortunately, you're right. But I'm seriously concerned about exposing you to a guy with these so-called deadly powers. What if he's a nut job?"

"Okay. I'll compromise," the president said with a grin. "I'll let you meet with him, and then if he decides to go on a killing spree, it'll be you, not me, who'll be his victim."

"I'm not sure that's a compromise, but maybe he'd be doing me a favor."

"Hey, don't talk that way. I'd be lost without your sound advice and wise counsel, so if you're struggling, let's talk about it and get you some help."

"Thanks, man. I appreciate that. I'm okay, but I've got a lot going on both here and at home."

"I understand, probably better than anyone else in your life, and I'm here for you. Never forget that. Now go figure out if this guy can throw the Hail Mary we need."

The intercom buzzed. "Special Agent Silver is here," a woman's voice said.

Emmitt stood up. "I'll take him into the conference room, and you stay here and watch the proceedings with your presidential spycam."

▲ ▼ ▲

"So, Special Agent Silver, any idea why you're here?" Emmitt asked.

"No, sir. When I spoke to the president on Christmas morning, he said he had an issue." Jake did his best to stifle a grin, but Emmitt noticed.

"What's so funny?"

"Nothing, sir, it's just that six months ago, I was a newly retired financial planner with no plans for the immediate future. Never in my wildest dreams could I have imagined that I'd become a special agent and the president of the United States would be calling me on Christmas morning."

"I understand. What's the old saying? 'Man plans and God laughs.' Now, according to several people for whom I have the utmost respect, you have a unique gift."

"Do you mean my Humphrey Bogart impersonation?"

"No, but I happen to love Bogie, and I'm pleased you have a sense of humor. I'm talking about your talent for eliminating problematic people and other creatures."

"Ah, that. Yes, I'm afraid I do have that gift, although some might say it's a curse."

"I would think it's both. But be honest. Could you actually point your finger at me right now and say, 'Just die,' and I'd croak?"

"Yes, sir. I believe I could. Would you like me to try it?"

"No, not today, thanks. I'm actually having a pretty good day. But the way things are going, maybe tomorrow. But let me ask you, aren't you ever tempted to use your gift, shall we say, indiscriminately?"

Jake frowned. "Nah, that would be stupid. But let me ask you. Do you own a handgun?"

"Yes, I do. I live in the District, so I keep it by my bedside for protection."

"So, are you ever tempted to use it indiscriminately?"

"That's a stupid question. Of course not."

"Well then, there you go. I have no interest in using my power for any purpose other than serving my country. And no offense, sir, but I thought I was meeting with the president."

"I'm sure you understand the risks involved with having someone with your talents meet the president in person," Emmitt replied. At that moment, the door opened. The president was standing in the doorway, grinning.

"Mr. Silver seems pretty trustworthy to me," the president said, and he motioned to Jake to follow him into the Oval

Office. He sat down at his desk, clasped his hands, and looked directly at Jake. "I'm going to cut to the chase, since my chief of staff used up all my time with you. As you know, I, along with a number of former presidents, have been working to get North Korea to denuclearize. While Kim Jong-un is amenable to the idea of giving up nuclear weapons, it appears he's being, hmm, let's say, thwarted by three young and very popular generals."

"I thought Kim Jong-un had complete control."

"No, unfortunately, he doesn't. He still controls the old guard and the old generals, and he's not shy about removing them as necessary. But times have changed, and he knows his people are starving as a result of the sanctions we've placed on his county. Even the Chinese, who can't even feed their own people, have started to cut off the food supply. And now he's being challenged by these imperious young generals who don't want him to give up the nukes, so he's asked us for assistance."

"Seriously?"

"Dead serious, no pun intended. He'd like us to eliminate the three generals, and, if possible, their assistant commanders. And until I heard about you, I had no idea how to make that happen."

Jake looked up at the ornate ceiling and sighed. "But how the heck would I be able to do that? Couldn't you send in a bunch of commandos armed to the teeth?"

"Believe me, I proposed that idea, along with a few others. But Kim Jong-un wants it done with no press, no violence, and no bloodshed. Which is why you, Mr. Silver, are the right man for the job."

The president's intercom buzzed. "Mr. President, your next appointment is here," a woman's voice said.

"I'll be right out. Jake, our time is up for today, but I look forward to seeing you when you return from your assignment. As I'm sure you understand, America, not to mention the rest of the free world, is counting on you. So read my mind and don't fuck this up."

38

THE NEXT TWO WEEKS WERE A blur. Jake flew back to Minneapolis, recounted the conversation to Beth Ann, and packed his bags. The next day, she drove him to the airport, and he flew back to Dulles. The same limo driver who picked him up before was waiting outside the airport. He greeted Jake and drove him to CIA headquarters in McLean, Virginia.

Jake's first order of business was a four-hour meeting with his handler, Richard "Dick" Payne. As soon as Jake shook Dick's hand, he knew they weren't destined to be lifelong buddies. Dick was tall and lanky with hair the color of a sewer rat, and he had sloped shoulders that made him look like a human question mark. He also had the strangest eyes Jake had ever seen. They were pale pink, with small red irises, and they seemed to look in different directions, giving him the appearance of a chameleon. Between his acne-scarred skin and a perpetual scowl, Dick gave off a negative energy that made Jake briefly consider offing him. But as he talked through the plan, Jake begrudgingly acknowledged that Dick knew his stuff.

As Dick explained, the three young North Korean generals and their assistant commanders had been meeting regularly in Nakhodka, Russia. An up-and-coming port city on the Trudny Peninsula, Nakhodka was 53 miles east of Vladivostok and less than an hour by plane from Pyongyang.

Jake scanned the intelligence reports and looked at dozens of photos, which revealed that the North Koreans favored a small boutique hotel on the ocean with a pool and nightclub. Led by an officer named General Kim Lee Park, the generals and their commanders were in meetings all day, but they always broke for cocktails and lunch with a cadre of local Russian hostesses. When the clock struck five, the hostesses went to the hotel, where they ate, drank, danced, and skinny-dipped with the officers until the wee hours.

According to Dick, he and Jake they would be flying to Vladivostok, where they'd be met by a driver and transported to Nakhodka. They would stay at a hotel owned by the same people who owned the boutique hotel. The next morning, Jake would be driven to the boutique hotel, where he would begin working as a waiter, which entailed serving the generals, their commanders, and the hostesses.

Dick informed Jake that he would be expected to kill everyone in the hotel, which gave Jake pause, since he was only willing to eliminate those individuals who threatened the safety of his country. He considered aborting the mission, but made up his mind to spare the civilians. Once the killing spree was over, Jake was to run out to the terrace, where one of Kim Jong-un's helicopters would be waiting to ferry him and Dick to a ship waiting in the Bay of Japan.

The next order of business was a series of Russian language lessons. But after the first two sessions, the instructor threw up his hands at Jake's nasal Midwestern accent and told him to speak as little as possible when he was in Nakhodka. He then pulled out a chess board. They played three games. Jake let him win the first round, but then proceeded to trounce him in the second and third. When the instructor asked Jake where he'd learned to play chess, he admitted that he'd been on the Stevens Point Area High School chess team.

▲ ▼ ▲

The trip to Vladivostok was easier than Jake had expected. Midway through the 13½ hour flight, the plane stopped in Frankfurt to refuel, but Jake didn't notice, since he was sleeping on a reclining bed in a private cubicle. When TJ learned that Jake and Dick would be flying coach to Russia, he'd upgraded Jake to first class. Dick wasn't too happy about it, but since Homeland Security was paying Jake's way, there was nothing he could do.

When they finally landed at Vladivostok International Airport, Dick and Jake were met at the gate by an American security officer with a golf cart. He navigated the throngs of people and whisked them to an idling Lada Kalina. The driver, an older Russian man, apparently did not speak a word of English, so the drive to Nakhodka was quiet.

They passed the boutique hotel where the North Koreans were staying and continued along the seafront. The driver stopped in front of a slightly seedier hotel. Dick and Jake retrieved their baggage from the trunk, carried it into the lobby, and waited for someone to greet them. When nobody appeared, Jake stepped up to the counter and rang the bell.

A minute later, a curtain parted, revealing the most gorgeous woman Jake had ever seen. She was tall, with long brunette hair, flawless skin, and dazzling white teeth.

"Good day and welcome. I am Fabiana Lavka, and you must be the Americans," she said in flawless British English.

Jake watched as Dick tried to smile and straighten his stooped shoulders. "Yes, we are, Miss Lavka. I'm Richard Payne, and this is my associate Jake Silver."

"Oh, please call me Fabiana, Mr. Payne. I have two rooms reserved for you and Mr. Silver. I will show them to you now." Dick elbowed Jake out of the way so he could walk behind Fabiana. They climbed two flights and turned down a narrow hallway. Fabiana unlocked the doors of two adjacent rooms and stepped aside. "Please make yourselves comfortable. Mr. Silver, I will be driving you to our other hotel tomorrow morning, so I will meet you in the lobby at 7 a.m. Mr. Payne, your breakfast will be served in our dining room at 7:30."

▲ ▼ ▲

The next morning, Fabiana met Jake in the lobby. She was wearing a deep purple, circa 1980s suit with a broad-shouldered jacket, a narrow, tight skirt, and black stiletto heels that made her look like a Joan Collins-turned-Bond girl. He could smell her perfume, a scent he remembered from his college days. All the Kappa women wore Angel by

Thierry Mugler, a cloying yet compelling mix of chocolate, vanilla, and patchouli.

She slid behind the wheel of a vintage red Porsche. Jake had barely buckled his seatbelt when she gunned the engine and turned onto the boulevard that led to the other hotel. Minutes later, she pulled up to the entrance and got out, leaving the keys in the car. Jake followed her into the hotel. She strode through the lobby and led him to a spacious modern kitchen outfitted with a wall of stainless-steel refrigerators and a massive commercial range. At the rear of the kitchen, a group of servers were standing around a long table filled with platters of food. A tall man in a white *toque* was pointing at each plate and talking in Russian while a Chinese woman translated his words.

Fabiana nodded at the chef and opened the door to a small office. She perched on the edge of the desk and crossed her long legs. Jake took the only seat, an ancient metal desk chair, and did his best to concentrate.

"Thank you for coming to Nakhodka, Mr. Silver," Fabiana said.

"Um, my pleasure. Please call me Jake."

"And then you may call me Fabiana."

"I can't say it as beautifully as you do, but I'll try. The name reminds me of Fabian Forte, the famous American heartthrob."

"Ah, yes, my mother had, how you say it, a mad crush on him, so as ridiculous as it may sound, I am named after him.

She also loved Elvis Presley, so I am grateful she decided to save that for my brother."

"Yes, you're definitely not an Elvis."

"And hopefully you're not a hound dog. Now, shall we get down to business?" She hopped off the desk and handed him a waiter's uniform from a hook on the wall. "You may change in the men's room, and then I will introduce you to the team."

Jake returned to her office with his civilian clothes under his arm. Fabiana closed the door, took the clothes, and put them on her desk. "Before we begin, I'd like to acknowledge your employer's generous contribution to our operation," she said quietly. "It has allowed us to invest in new equipment and hire a new chef who will elevate our cuisine and put this hotel on the map, so to speak. I will now introduce you to the team. I have explained that you are an old friend from my college days in London. You are opening an Asian-fusion restaurant in America, and you are here to learn how we create our signature brand of hospitality. I have used a portion of your employer's money to give them each a $100 bonus for helping you learn how to be a waiter."

"Sounds good to me. I'm happy that my boss was able to help you."

Fabiana opened the door and led him over to a table where the chef was working. She put her hand on the chef's shoulder and said a few words in Russian. The chef nodded and said something to the waiters and waitresses. They looked at Fabiana expectantly, and she began to speak. She put her hand on Jake's elbow and pointed to each person as she introduced them, first in Russian and then in English. When she reached a young, handsome man, she said, "And this is my brother, Elvis Lavka, named after you-know-who."

"Nice to meet you all," Jake said. "Thank you for helping me become a waiter." Fabiana translated his words into Russian, and the translator repeated them in Chinese.

"While they are finishing with their tasting, I will introduce you to our accountant, and then we will come back here so you can help with the lunch shift," Fabiana said. "Come with me."

Jake had imagined the accountant would be a short, squat bean-keeper of a man in an ill-fitting brown suit. To his surprise, he saw a young woman with cropped hair, no makeup, and a gold tooth. "Jake, I would like you to meet our accountant and my fiancée, Misha Mikahilov." Fabiana put her arm around the woman's sturdy shoulders.

"Nice to meet you, Misha," Jake said, all thoughts of a brown-suited accountant vanishing from his mind. "If you don't mind me asking, when are you two getting married?"

"Well, now that we have gotten a wonderful chef on board, we are planning our wedding for June 21, the longest day of the year."

"Congratulations! I also have a fiancée. Her name is Beth Ann, and she's beautiful and smart. She's studying to be a veterinarian. We haven't picked a date yet for our wedding, but I'm hoping it will be sometime this year."

"Perhaps we could have a double wedding," Fabiana said.

"That would be cool," Misha said. "I can tell that we are going to get along like a house on fire, as you would say."

"Yes, and should you need any help with a diamond for your bride, my brother Alexei can help you," Fabiana said. "He has some very good connections in Yakutia."

"Thanks, I'll keep that in mind," Jake replied.

"But now we must get back to the kitchen," Fabiana said. "Our guests will be assembling in the lounge in a few minutes. They will be having cocktails and appetizers, and then they will move into the dining room for lunch."

Fabiana and Jake walked quickly back down the hallway. "I think Misha was right when she said we will become good friends," she whispered. "Perhaps you can help us get out of Russia, where people like Misha and I are not welcome."

She pushed open the door to the kitchen. Inside, a sous-chef handed Jake a platter of chilled shrimp and motioned him to follow another waiter with a tray of *blini* and caviar. The waiter pushed open another door with his elbow, and Jake followed into a lounge where the guests were gathered.

"Just do what I do," the waiter whispered in fractured English. He walked up to a man in a military uniform and bowed. The man examined the tray of *blini*, took one, and popped the whole thing in his mouth. He took a second blini and then turned to Jake. He took the biggest shrimp, dunked it in a ramekin of cocktail sauce, and ate it in one bite. He pulled the tail out of his mouth, dropped it on Jake's tray, turned on his heel, and stalked away.

Jake followed the waiter around the room as he deftly navigated the crowd, proffering the appetizers to each guest. Jake quickly determined which men were the generals and their underlings. He tried to count the number of hostesses, but quickly lost count, since there were dozens of them, each leggier and more beautiful than the next. When Jake's tray was empty, he made his way back to the kitchen, where the sous-chef handed him a tray of crostini topped with a slice of rare prime rib and a dab of horseradish *crème fraîche.*

▲ ▼ ▲

When Jake returned to the lounge, he noticed a handsome North Korean officer conversing in fluent Russian with one of the hostesses. The man must have said something funny, because the woman blushed and started giggling. The officer looked directly at Jake and nodded in recognition, which gave Jake pause, as he didn't remember seeing the man's face in the dossier. Jake nodded politely and walked toward the door. He pushed it open and stood in the hallway. After making sure nobody was in earshot, he pulled a satellite phone out of his pocket and pressed a button.

"Speak," a gruff Korean voice said.

"Go," Jake replied.

"Twelve minutes," the voice said, and hung up.

Jake took a deep breath and slipped the phone back into his pocket. He went back into the lounge and scanned the room. He turned toward one of the generals, who was chatting with the tallest and blondest of the hostesses. Jake lifted his right hand, pointed his index finger at the general, and whispered, "Just die."

The general pitched forward, his head landing face down in the hostess's cleavage. His cocktail glass crashed to the floor, sending ice cubes and jagged shards of crystal flying as the hostess started screaming. Wasting no time, Jake pointed his finger at the second general, then the third.

As the men collapsed like dominoes, the women ran for the doors, and the waiters dropped their trays and tried to stop them from leaving. By this time, the generals' adjuncts had pulled their pistols and were spinning in circles, looking in vain for the assailants. Jake pointed his hand at the adjuncts and fluttered his fingers as if he were waving from a float in the Macy's Thanksgiving parade. He whispered "Just die" three times, and the men crumpled and fell lifeless to the floor.

Jake heard a shot and turned toward the sound. At that instant, he felt a tug on his upper arm. He looked down. The sleeve of his white waiter's jacket was turning crimson with blood gushing from a wound. Feeling like he was about to faint, he looked up and saw General Kim Lee Park pointing a pistol at his forehead. A second bullet screamed past his ear, and as he fell to the floor, he saw Misha plunge a chef's knife into the back of the general's neck. Jake lay on the floor, his head spinning. He watched as the officer fell backwards onto the knife, pushing it so far into his neck that it came out the other side.

Misha knelt down by Jake's side, and one of the waiters handed her a white napkin. She made a tourniquet and held it firmly in place. The waiter helped Misha lift Jake to his feet and prop his uninjured arm around her shoulders. By this time, Jake could hear the sounds of a helicopter outside, so he mustered up all his strength.

"I think my ride is here," he said to Misha. She nodded and helped him limp toward the French doors that opened on to the terrace. Fabiana and the handsome North Korean officer were waiting with their hands extended to help Jake step outside.

"Before you point that finger of yours at me, you should know I'm one of the good guys," the officer said to Jake. He smiled, and the officer, Fabiana, and Misha helped him climb into the helicopter. Dick Payne was already inside. He nodded at the officer, then frowned at Fabiana and Misha, but said nothing. The women got Jake settled in his seat and then sat down and buckled their seatbelts. As the helicopter gained altitude, they could see a cavalcade of police cars tearing down the avenue, sirens wailing and lights flashing.

"Thanks again for the help," Jake said to the officer.

"Y'all are welcome," the officer replied in English with a Southern accent. "Glad to help."

"What the hell? Did you just say y'all?"

"Sho 'nuff. I played baseball at Louisiana."

"No shit?" Jake pointed his finger at the officer, who flinched.

"Go Tigers, beat 'Bama!" Jake said, and everyone except Dick started laughing.

▲ ▼ ▲

Dick was pissed. He was not expecting Fabiana, let alone her lover, to jump into the helicopter. He'd never anticipated that Fabiana would be such a looker, so after she'd taken him and Jake up to their hotel rooms, he'd waited for ten or so minutes and then slipped back downstairs in search of her. He found her at the bar having a glass of wine and sat down next to her. Well-versed in the behaviors of American men, she offered him a drink and quietly reminded him of their professional working relationship. She then informed him she was a lesbian. Dick was mortified and morally outraged. A born-again Christian from Greenville, South Carolina, he was shocked when beautiful women made the choice to be lesbians—at least he assumed it was a choice.

Dick was also outraged with Jake. He sat in his seat shaking with anger and cursing silently as he replayed the events in the lounge. There was only one reason Da Boss had recruited Jake for the mission, and that was because Kim Jong-un did not want any violence, gunplay, or bloodshed. The fact that General Kim Lee Park was the one who fired his handgun was lost on Dick. He was also disgusted with Jake's inability to follow instructions, since

Dick had specifically directed Jake to kill everyone in the room. *If he'd goddamn listened to me, Misha would be dead, and maybe Fabiana would change her mind about me.*

He gave Jake a withering glance. "Hey, Jake, glad you're still with us. Too bad you didn't follow my instructions. As you'll remember, this mission was never supposed to involve violence or bloodshed. And if you'd followed directions, you'd never have fainted. For a so-called special agent, you're a wussy and a total lightweight. Having heard about your issues with blood, I'm surprised you didn't puke all over the floor. Un-freaking-believable."

"Listen, Dick, why don't y'all give it a rest and sit back and enjoy the ride?" the North Korean officer said. "Jake never touched a gun and, by all accounts, he's a hero. I've already texted your people to let them know that the mission was a success."

"Well, that remains to be seen," Dick snarled. "As far as I'm concerned, Jake's a loose cannon and, if it were up to me, I'd revoke his privileges and make sure he never lends his so-called special powers to another CIA initiative. We could have done this without him."

Jake glared at Dick. "A loose cannon, huh?" He raised his first finger.

Dick's eyes widened. "You can't do this."

"I most certainly could," Jake said, clasping his hands in his lap. "But lucky for you, I won't. Just so long as you stay away from me."

"Two minutes to touchdown," the pilot called out. He began maneuvering for a landing on a huge cargo ship.

"Before we land, I'd like to say something," the Korean officer said. "Kim Jong-un is my uncle, and I know he's pleased with what transpired today. I also knew General Kim Lee Park and all the generals and their adjuncts. I'm sorry they're dead, but they cared nothing about humanity. They were willing to fight to the death for nuclear weapons." He looked at Jake, Fabiana, and Misha and grinned. "Karma's a bitch, right?"

The helicopter landed on the tarmac and the door slid open. A uniformed officer greeted them. "I'm Captain Genovese. Welcome to my ship," the man said. "Especially you, my friend." He nodded at the North Korean officer.

"Permission to come aboard, Captain?" The officer jumped onto the deck.

"Permission granted!" Genovese replied and slapped him on the back.

Dick went next, then Misha and Fabiana helped Jake down the stairs. The North Korean held up his phone. "Smile, Jake. This one's for my uncle."

39

GINO AND HIS SISTER MARY WERE at the Varsity Theater in St. Paul. He rarely took a night off, but since Mary's life partner Leslie Scarmuzzo and her band Retro Groove were performing live, he made an exception. Gino loved Leslie's voice because she sounded exactly like Linda Ronstadt.

Leslie looked out into her audience. "This one's for my favorite brother-in-law," she said. She nodded to her bandmates, and they broke into "Blue Bayou," Gino's all-time favorite song. Mary put her hand on his arm, and he let her keep it there for the entire song.

Before the concert, Gino and Mary had met for dinner at the Red Rabbit on Grand Avenue. Over a bottle of chianti and a platter of chicken parmesan, Gino unloaded on Mary. A gifted psychologist, Mary had watched Gino's marriage unravel, and she was relieved he'd finally decided to share his struggles with her. When he confessed that he'd neglected his family in the pursuit of the police chief position, Mary nodded. While she didn't share her brother's rabid ambition, she understood his desire for the top job, so she let him pour his heart out. "And that's why she's divorcing me," he said, his voice breaking. "I can't say I blame her."

"Oh, Gino, it'll be okay. Maybe not today, but eventually. For right now, stop beating yourself up, and let's go hear some good music."

▲ ▼ ▲

"What do you mean you didn't put the morphine syringe in the evidence locker?" Gino looked at George's bloodshot eyes and sighed. "What the hell did you do with it?"

George hung his head and tried to think, but it was difficult, since he was high. Ever since he'd confiscated that syringe from DC Krueger, he'd been hooked on morphine. He'd recently switched to heroin, because it was easier to get from his network of drug dealers, especially when he threatened them with jail time if they ever told anyone.

"Goddamn it, Burnsey," Gino said, "you're higher than a kite. Don't tell me you're using."

"Okay, I won't," George said with a foolish grin.

"Oh, for Chrissakes. Take off your coat and roll up your sleeves." Gino helped George take off his sport coat and unbutton his cuffs. George pushed up his sleeves, and Gino whistled as he stared at the tracks on his arms. "Jesus Christ, Burnsey. You're in way over your head. What the hell have you been using?"

"Oh, a little heroin, a little meth, and a little snort of cocaine here and there. You should try it sometime. Sure beats chasing the goddamn captain's job and working yourself to death."

"I'm not so sure about that, Burnsey. Put your coat back on. I'm marching you over to the captain's office so he can decide what to do with you."

As Gino had anticipated, Captain Les Becker took one look at George's arms and immediately confiscated his badge, his gun, and the keys to his ancient police car. But instead of throwing George into a jail cell, he told Gino to drive him home. Gino followed George into his apartment and did a cursory sweep of the place. There were a couple empty syringes and a cigar box with a single dried-out cigar on the coffee table. The fridge was empty, save a half-empty bottle of orange juice. Gino handed George two twenty-dollar bills, told him to order a pizza, and left.

▲ ▼ ▲

Instead of going back to work, Gino drove to his former home. He looked longingly at the house. Neither big nor small, it was just right for a family of four, and he had loved living there. He noticed the brick pathway was crumbling and the siding needed repair. He rang the doorbell and waited.

"Just a minute!" His wife's voice echoed from the hallway. She opened the door and sucked in her breath. "What's going on, Gino? Shouldn't you be at work chasing the captain's job?"

"Vicki, hear me out. I'm not at work because I'm here to apologize for everything. I've been an idiot, and I'm truly sorry for putting my job before you and the kids."

Victoria began to sway, and Gino grabbed her before she fainted. He carried her into the living room and set her gently on the sofa. It was the first piece of furniture they'd bought together. He went into the kitchen and filled a glass with water. He handed it to her, and she took a sip. "Am I dreaming?" she asked with a smile.

"No, my darling Vicki, you're not dreaming. I'm so sorry, my love. I put my career ahead of my family, and I'm here to tell you it will never happen again."

"Oh, Gino, if you're asking me if I forgive you, the answer is yes, as long as you really mean it."

"I mean it with all my heart. Cross my chest and hope to die if I'm lying to you."

"I'm not sure that's the way you say it, but I get your intention. And if I know one thing about you, Gino Sweeney, you're not a liar, so welcome home, my darling, welcome home."

▲ ▼ ▲

George called Domino's and ordered a large, thick-crust pepperoni pizza. Then he sat down on his threadbare sofa, opened the cigar box, and took out the lone cigar. With shaking hands, he unwrapped it, lit the end without clipping it, and took a few greedy puffs. His stomach heaved, and he vomited a puddle of yellow bile onto the table. He slid to the floor and curled up in a ball, shaking and shivering. Minutes went by, and he finally sat up. Leaning against the sofa, he reached for his throwaway gun and raised it to his temple. "Lord Jesus, I accept you as my savior. Please forgive me," he whispered, and squeezed the trigger.

40

IT WAS DC'S LAST DAY AT Hazelden, and she was sitting in Dr. de Castro's office. "Your son Lawrence and I have been collaborating on a children's book," DC said. She handed the doctor a thick file folder. "These are the illustrations that I promised him."

"Mind if I have a look?"

DC nodded.

The doctor opened the folder. "My gosh, DC, these drawings are absolutely wonderful!"

"Really?" DC's eyes sparkled. "You really like them?"

"Oh, my dear, I love them. You are so talented. Have you always been an artist?"

"I always loved drawing as a kid, but then I got hooked on drugs, so I forgot about art. As soon as I quit doing drugs, my passion just came bubbling back."

"Well, you have a real gift. I'll give your drawings to Lawrence, and he'll be so pleased. I'll also make sure he gives you credit when the book is published. Did he ever share with you how he discovered his writing ability?"

"Yes, he did. He said he used to be an addict like me. When he went through recovery, he realized he needed something to replace the booze, so he started re-reading the books he loved when he was a kid, which led him to want to write his own books for kids."

"Lawrence probably also told you how he found God."

"Yes, he did. He even inspired me to learn about Jesus, and I really think it's helping me stay sober."

"Oh, DC, I'm so happy for you. I'm so glad you and Lawrence are friends, and I hope you'll keep in touch with him—and me. Now I believe your friend Tim is picking you up, so I'll walk you out."

"My God, DC, you look fabulous!" Tim said.

"Thanks, Tim. I feel great! Where's Jamie?"

"He's in the car. I wanted to give you a heads-up. We got married last week, so we're now husband and husband."

"Oh, Tim, that's so wonderful. I'm so happy for you."

"Thank you, DC. I hope my letter didn't shock you. I wasn't sure if you knew I was gay, so I wanted to make sure before I introduced you to Jamie."

"To be honest, I was a little disappointed, you handsome devil. But I too have found the love of my life. His name is Lawrence, and I'm already dreaming about our honeymoon in Paris!"

▲ ▼ ▲

Beth Ann spun around in front of the mirror, and her mother clapped her hands. "Oh, Beth Ann," she said. "I'm so glad we came to Posh Bridal Couture first. We don't need to go to any other salon. That gown is so gorgeous on you. You'll be the most beautiful bride."

Beth Ann stopped spinning and looked at herself. She was wearing the pearls that Jake had given her, and they were the same luminous ivory as the dress. The silhouette was a simple sheath that made the most of her figure, and even without tailoring, it fit her perfectly. "I absolutely love it, but it's so expensive. It's way out of our price range."

"What the hell!" her mother said. "Think of it as a wedding gift from your asshole father, since it's his life insurance that's paying for it."

"Thank you, Mom. I think Jake will love it."

"How could he not?" Cindy Swenson, the salesperson, said. "You look positively regal."

41

JAKE AND OMAR WERE SITTING around the campfire at the Fleischauers' cabin. It was the weekend before Memorial Day, and Beth Ann had a bridal shower, so she'd stayed home. The Loon Saloon was closed, so Jake put a couple of pizzas in the oven and set the timer on his cell phone. When the phone beeped, Omar stood up. "I'll get the pizzas if you grab more firewood."

Jake got an armful of wood from the stack. He was just about to toss a couple of logs into the firepit when he felt a piece of hard metal against the back of his head.

"Put your hands behind you, or I'll blow your head off," a familiar voice said. "Do it now!"

Jake put his hands behind him, and the man quickly fastened a pair of handcuffs around Jake's wrists and stuffed a handkerchief into his mouth. "Now turn around," the voice said. Jake turned slowly around to see Dick Payne with a Glock in his hand.

"Well, Special Agent Silver, I guess we meet again," he said. "Nice digs. Too bad you won't be enjoying this hideaway anymore." Dick slid his other hand into his jacket and pulled out a leather holder. He flipped it open and showed it to Jake. "See this? They took away my badge and demoted me. They even took my gun away. Said I didn't need it to ride a desk."

Dick waved the Glock at Jake. "But I don't need their freaking gun. I've got enough of my own to outfit a small platoon. This Glock here is one of my favorites. I chose it especially for you, Jake. Which is too bad, since I'll be throwing it in the lake after you're dead. But what the hell. Only the best for you, Special Agent Silver. Now how does it feel to be the one without any power? Go ahead and point your finger at me and say, 'Just die.' You can't, can you?"

Dick waved the gun at Jake again. "You know, Jake, I made a big mistake. When we got back from Nakhodka, I called the president and told him how you got us involved in a bloody mess. Instead of thanking me, he put me on hold. Next thing I know, I'm talking to the chief of staff, and he tells me I'm being pulled from the field. Now I'm a glorified paper jockey with a salary I can barely live on. But what the fuck, Jake, shit happens, and right now, it's happening to you. Say goodbye to the world, Jake." Dick kissed his gun on the muzzle, raised it slowly, pointed it at Jake's forehead, and whispered, "Just..."

A shot rang out. Dick's ugly mug exploded, and his gun fell to the ground.

"Like I always say, Silverado, the gun gives me options," Omar called out from the deck. "Now come on up for dinner. The pizza's getting cold."

Omar unlocked Jake's handcuffs and tossed them on the table. Jake called TJ and told him what happened. Within minutes, his phone rang. It was Chief John Michaud.

"I talked to TJ," John said. "You and Omar stay where you are. I'm on my way over with my deputy Steve Dalton."

Jake and Omar saved half a pizza for John and went out to the deck to wait for him. Soon, they heard car doors slamming. John came around the back of the cabin and down the hill, followed by Steve, who was pushing a wheelbarrow with a tarp in it.

John looked at Dick's near-headless body and walked up the stairs to the deck. "Good work for a football player," John said, and fist-bumped Omar. He went inside, took a beer from the fridge, and helped himself to the pizza. He came back outside and sat down in a chair, watching Steve as he pushed the wheelbarrow up to Dick's body.

"Whoa, somebody's not having a good day," Steve said. He took a stick from the fire and burned the fingerprints off Dick's hands. Then he poked the stick into the remains of Dick's mouth. "Nice work, Omar. No dental work left to identify him. What the hell did you shoot him with?"

"Just a SIG Sauer," Omar replied with a laugh. He helped Steve wrap Dick in the tarp, and they swung the bundle into the wheelbarrow and pushed it up the hill.

"Where's Steve taking Dick?" Jake asked.

"Where else but the town dump? After all, bears gotta eat, right? Otherwise, they... just die!"

The End

Acknowledgements

First of all, I would like to acknowledge you, the reader. I am grateful that you dedicated your valuable time to reading my novel.

Thanks also to my editor and friend Melinda Nelson for all her great work in shaping and polishing *Just Die;* to Ken Schubert for formatting and managing production; and to Lynn Cross, the world's best copy editor and proofreader.

And finally, thanks and love to my wife Paula. She is a great editor, proofreader, and most of all a wonderful wife.

Peace,

EAF

About the Author

E. Alan Fleischauer is the author of eight books to date. His first, *Rescued,* launched the acclaimed JT Thomas series and was awarded Chanticleer International's Laramie Award First Prize for best traditional western of 2019. The follow-on novels *Hunted* and *Kidnapped* were published in 2020, and next books in the series, *Tommies* and *JT's World,* will be released in 2021.

Mr. Fleischauer has also published a book of short stories entitled *Just Another Morning,* centered on U.S. holidays or special events. The title story chronicles a woman's harrowing ordeal in the World Trade Center on September 11, 2001.

His picture book *Charlie Lou goes to the Rodeo* was inspired by the birth of his granddaughter. Mr. Fleischauer hopes that this book will create awareness about autism.

His poem *Suicide Is Forever* was awarded First Prize in the 2020 contest sponsored by Two Sisters Publishing.

Alan is now writing *Sherlock and the Tiger,* a detective novel to be released in 2022.

Alan lives in Victoria, Minnesota with his wife Paula. His books are available on Amazon.

Also by E.A. Fleischauer

RESCUED
#1 in the JT Thomas Saga

HUNTED
#2 in the JT Thomas Saga

KIDNAPPED
#3 in the JT Thomas Saga

JUST ANOTHER MORNING
A Collection of Short Stories

Soon to come

TOMMIES
A Western Detective Series

JT'S WORLD
#4 in the JT Thomas Saga

CHARLIE LOU GOES TO THE RODEO
A Children's Picture Book

SHERLOCK AND THE TIGER
A Detective Novel